FAVORITES FROM CHRIS GRABENSTEIN

The Island of Dr. Libris
No More Naps!
Shine! (coauthored with J.J. Grabenstein)

MR. LEMONCELLO'S LIBRARY SERIES

Mr. Lemoncello's Very First Game
Escape from Mr. Lemoncello's Library
Mr. Lemoncello's Library Olympics
Mr. Lemoncello's Great Library Race
Mr. Lemoncello's All-Star Breakout Game
Mr. Lemoncello and the Titanium Ticket

THE SMARTEST KID IN THE UNIVERSE SERIES

The Smartest Kid in the Universe
Genius Camp

DOG SQUAD SERIES

Dog Squad
Cat Crew

WELCOME TO WONDERLAND SERIES

Home Sweet Motel
Beach Party Surf Monkey
Sandapalooza Shake-Up
Beach Battle Blowout

HAUNTED MYSTERY SERIES

The Crossroads
The Demons' Door
The Zombie Awakening
The Black Heart Crypt

COAUTHORED WITH JAMES PATTERSON

Best Nerds Forever
The House of Robots series
The I Funny series
The Jacky Ha-Ha series
Katt vs. Dogg
The Max Einstein series
Pottymouth and Stoopid
Scaredy Cat
The Treasure Hunters series
Word of Mouse

CHRIS GRABENSTEIN

ILLUSTRATIONS BY BETH HUGHES

RANDOM HOUSE 🏠 NEW YORK

Text copyright © 2022 by Chris Grabenstein
Jacket art and interior illustrations copyright © 2022 by Beth Hughes

Visit us on the Web! rhcbooks.com

Educators and librarians, for a variety of teaching tools, visit us at RHTeachersLibrarians.com

Library of Congress Cataloging-in-Publication Data
Names: Grabenstein, Chris, author. | Hughes, Beth, artist.
Title: Cat crew / Chris Grabenstein; with art by Beth Hughes.
Description: New York: Random House Children's Books, 2022. | Series: Dog squad; 2 | Audience: Ages 8–12 | Summary: "Fred, a stray dog who became the star of the show *Dog Squad,* is working on a new show called *Cat Crew,* but when he notices the felines acting strange, he wonders if the cat crew is being electronically controlled"—Provided by publisher.
Identifiers: LCCN 2021043970 | ISBN 978-0-593-48087-8 (hardcover) | ISBN 978-0-593-48088-5 (library binding) | ISBN 978-0-593-64487-4 (int'l) | ISBN 978-0-593-48090-8 (ebook)
Subjects: CYAC: Dogs—Fiction. | Cats—Fiction. | Adventure and Adventurers—Fiction. | Television—Production and direction—Fiction.
Classification: LCC PZ7.G7487 Cat 2022 | DDC [Fic]—dc23

Printed in the United States of America
10 9 8 7 6 5 4 3 2 1
First Edition

FOR J.J., THE CAT WHISPERER, AND OUR CAT CREW,
PAST AND PRESENT: JEANETTE, WILLOW, PARKER,
TIGER LILLY, PHOEBE SQUEAK, AND LUIGI

DOG SQUAD

EPISODE 3.15

"EIFFEL TERRIBLE"

SCENE 24

Ext. the top of the Eiffel Tower.

THE DIABOLICAL VILLAIN known as Catty-wampus has stepped in one too many piles of dog poop on the sidewalks of Paris. It has made his soul bitter. His shoes stinky.

Cattywampus has vowed to eliminate all the dogs in Paris by turning the sight-seeing telescopes on the observation deck of the 1,063-foot-tall iron tower into dog-seeking sizzle guns.

"It's time to grill the hot dogs!" he

shouts to his minions, a brigade of Parisian alley cats who despise dogs even more than Cattywampus does.

The cats meow maniacally and leap up to their perches on the high-tech weapons. They wrap their claws around the triggers, awaiting the signal to fire.

Meanwhile, the Dog Squad—Duke, Nala, and Scruffy—continues its mad dash up the 1,665 steps to the top of the Eiffel Tower.

"Nothing's . . . too . . . ruff . . . for . . . us," pants Scruffy, the crew's scrappy, wisecracking terrier.

"This is pawful, Duke," says Nala, the world's bravest and boldest border collie. "Those beams will French-fry every dog on both sides of the Seine!"

"And *we're* dogs!" barks Scruffy. "I don't want to be fried to a crispity crunch!"

"Well, mes amis," says their heroic leader, Duke, his noble head rimmed with golden light, "when trouble calls . . ."

The three canine crusaders pause their ascent to proudly proclaim, "It's Dog Squad to the rescue!"

Suddenly, a wild-eyed mass of tangled fur leaps out of the shadows with its curled claws extended.

"Yipes!" yips Scruffy. "Cat attack!"

"You two deal with these henchcats," says Duke, hurtling up the staircase. "I'll deal with Cattywampus on my own!"

Meanwhile, at the top of the Eiffel Tower . . .

The ray guns thrum as they gain power.

"When do we destroy all the dogs?" hisses an angry cat.

"Soon, my fine furry friends," chortles Cattywampus, rubbing his mittened hands together. "Soon!"

"How do we know we won't accidentally hurt any cats?" asks a fraidy-cat dangling off one of the weapons.

"Don't get hiss-terical, Monsieur Fromage! I have designed these weapons purrfectly. They will target only dogs."

"Wait just a doggone minute!" shouts Duke, leaping onto the observation deck.

"Drat!" snarls the villain in his thick French accent. "It is Duke. The heroic leader of the Dog Squad. He thinks he can save the world! 'Ha!' I say. Go home to America, you filthy fleabag!"

"Sir," says Duke, "I don't like your cat-titude!"

Duke races around the deck, barking ferociously, scaring the evil minions, who turn tail and flee. Cattywampus can do nothing but shake his mittened fist at the sky.

As the ray guns power down, the cats seek safety by climbing the tallest thing they can find: the antenna at the peak of the Eiffel Tower. Their fur slightly ruffled, Nala and Scruffy join Duke on the observation deck.

"Looks like you treed those kitties just in time!" says Nala.

"Guess somebody better call the fire department to come rescue 'em," cracks Scruffy.

"No," says Duke nobly. "We will assist these cats

6

in their descent, just as soon as we deliver Cattywampus to the proper authorities. For they aren't bad cats. They simply
wound up in the wrong furever home."

The music swells.

The scene ends.

The audience cheers.

"AND CUT!" CALLED the director. "That's a wrap for this location and a wrap for Paris. We're heading home!"

The film crew applauded and congratulated each other.

"Good job, mes amis," said the French actor playing Cattywampus, giving Fred, Nala, and Scruffy each a head pat. "It was an honor to work with you."

Fred played Duke, the beloved leader of the number one streaming sensation, *Dog Squad*. Nala and Scruffy had been with the show from the start. Fred had only joined the cast about six months ago. He took over for the original Duke, who could've been Fred's identical twin (except that the lightning bolts of white fur on their foreheads slashed in opposite directions).

Sometimes Fred couldn't believe what an incredible journey his life had been. From an abandoned, unloved stray searching for scraps of food in an alley to a star in less than a year.

People all over the globe cheered the heart-racing, tail-wagging adventures of Scruffy, Nala, and their fearless leader, Duke.

But now, when the cameras and lights were off, Fred didn't feel like Duke. He was just Fred. A dog perched at the top of the Eiffel Tower in Paris, his legs quivering. He wanted to close his eyes because he was up SOOOO high, and Fred, it turned out, was SOOOO afraid of heights.

"Hey, Fred," said Scruffy. "What's wrong, pal?"

"I've never been up this high before!" Fred admitted.

"Yes you have," said Nala. "Yesterday. When we filmed the first half of this sequence."

"But yesterday, I was Duke. When I'm pretending to be Duke, I can pretend to be brave. But now? You heard the director. It's a wrap. We're all done. I'm not Duke anymore. I'm just Fred."

His limbs shook so violently, Fred feared he might rattle the tower's girders loose and make all their rivets pop out. The whole Eiffel Tower could fly apart and tumble to the ground!

Eep! He hoped he didn't faint.

Jenny Yen, the famous animal trainer who had adopted Fred, Nala, and Scruffy (and more than three dozen other talented dogs), came over with a fanny pack full of treats.

Scruffy gobbled his down in a flash. Nala sat in a confident pose and waited patiently for Jenny to present the treat in her palm.

"There is power in pausing," Nala said calmly. "And wisdom in waiting."

Scruffy rolled his eyes. Nala spent her off-seasons herding goats at a goat yoga retreat.

"You were such a good boy," Jenny said to Fred, "you deserve *two* treats."

But Fred wasn't hungry. In fact, just the thought of eating THIS HIGH OFF THE GROUND made his stomach lurch. His tail drooped.

"Wow," said Jenny. "Looks like somebody's pooped."

She turned to the crew.

"You guys? Let's get these three downstairs. They're worn out."

"No wonder," said the director. "They were awesome!"

"No," said Leo Espinosa, the show's writer and producer. "They were pawsome!"

Jenny clipped a leash onto Fred's collar and led him to

the elevator landing. One of her assistants escorted Nala and Scruffy.

Fred dared to look down. At Paris. The people looked like ants. The cars like beetles. His legs went all wobbly again.

Fred would need to ride two different elevators to make it down to the street. One from the top to a floor with a restaurant and more panoramic views. Another from that floor to the ground-level exit.

Both elevator cars were open cages! You could see everything as you flew up or plummeted down.

Fred closed his eyes.

And wished he was already home.

He loved his home at Jenny's ranch.

It was the best he'd ever had.

He'd do anything to keep living there.

But he'd rather not do any of it 984 feet above the ground.

PARIS WAS ONE of the dog-friendliest cities in the world.

Dogs were allowed in almost any store, shop, or restaurant, including the Restaurant Le Bouledogue, the café where the mascot, an elderly French bulldog, greeted Fred, Nala, and Scruffy when Jenny and Mr. Espinosa took them out on the town to "celebrate our Parisian triumph."

"Bonjour," said the gruff little bulldog. "I am, how you say, a very large fan of your work."

Then he kiss-licked all three on both cheeks.

"Um, thanks," said Fred.

"Merci," added Nala.

"You guys serve that steak with tartar sauce I've heard so much about?" asked Scruffy.

"You mean, of course, the steak tartare. Raw minced beef with onions, capers, and Worcestershire sauce."

"Yeah," said Scruffy. "I'm gonna have some of that. But without any onions, capers, or what's-this-here sauce. Just gimme the minced beef."

Fred was feeling better. For one thing, he was at street level. For another, he was with his best buds and two of his favorite humans in the world.

It was a beautiful night. Accordion music wafted on the breeze. The streetlights were twinkly. From his seat, Fred could see a TV playing behind the busy bar.

Escouade des chiens, which was French for *Dog Squad,* was on the screen. Human actors, of course, always dubbed in the voices for Duke, Nala, Scruffy, and all the other animal characters. Fred smiled. He had never heard himself speaking French before.

When the garçon (which Fred learned meant "waiter") came to the table, Jenny (who, of course, only heard barks when the dogs talked) somehow knew to order steak tartare for Scruffy, regular steak for Fred, and a "mélange of three fishes served with steamed seaweed" for Nala. Maybe Jenny's niece, Abby, got her "pet psychic" mind-reading capabilities from her aunt. Or maybe they both just got lucky sometimes.

Several other diners recognized the *Dog Squad* stars and asked for pawtographs, which the three dogs gladly provided. Jenny always packed an ink pad in her bag for just such requests.

Jenny and Mr. Espinosa clinked glasses filled with a

bubbly beverage and congratulated everyone, dogs included, on *Dog Squad*'s "terrific third season."

"Now we get to take a two-month break," said Mr. Espinosa with a contented sigh. "Any plans?"

"Just more of the same," said Jenny. "I'd like to expand the ranch a little so Abby and I can take in even more strays. Help them find their furever homes. Somebody abandoned all those puppies at the shelter during Hurricane Adelaide. . . ."

Mr. Espinosa smiled and shook his head. "You know you can't save the whole world all by yourself, Jenny."

"I know, I know," she said with a laugh. "So, when I need your help . . ."

Mr. Espinosa laughed. "Just ask for it."

"Thank you. I will."

"Is Nala spending her break at that goat yoga place again?"

Jenny nodded. "She loves it there."

"Can I take Scruffy home to Brooklyn for a few weeks?" said Mr. Espinosa. "We always have fun hanging out together."

"That sounds terrific," said Jenny.

"Yeah," said Scruffy between slurps of chopped meat. "I could use a little street time in New York City. It helps me maintain my edge, know what I mean?"

"Oh, indeed I do," said Nala.

Fred was wondering where he might spend what the TV people called the "hiatus." It meant a pause. A vacation. A little time off between wrapping up season three and the start of production for season four.

The break meant Fred could just be a dog and not a superhero for a little while. He'd like that!

Hmmmm, he thought. *Maybe I'll even chase a few cats up a few trees!*

MEANWHILE, BACK HOME in the United States, Jenny's twelve-year-old niece, Abby, was filling in for Jenny and the show's biggest stars at the Coastal Animal Shelter's annual gala.

The Wilford, Connecticut, charity held its major fundraiser of the year in a large party tent set up on the beach across the street from their shelter. Several dogs, wearing ADOPT ME vests, were being led by volunteers through the crowd, hoping to find their furever homes.

Abby had brought Tater Tot, a puppy rescued from the shelter, with her to the very posh event. Tater was another "wags-to-riches" story. After appearing in a few episodes, he had quickly become one of *Dog Squad*'s most popular new cast members.

"Hiya, folks!" Tater yipped as Abby stepped up to a brightly lit podium with the puppy cradled in her arms.

The audience went "Awwwww!" Tater's yips were awfully cute.

Abby was at the event to accept a Pawscar Award for all the good work being done by Jenny Yen's Second Chance Ranch. That was where Abby and her aunt rescued animals, trained some for film and stage, and found loving homes for all sorts of dogs, cats, and other animals.

"On behalf of my aunt Jenny and all the dogs in *Dog Squad*, I want to thank everybody at the Coastal Animal Shelter for doing what you do. I just talked to my aunt in Paris, where they're working on this season's final show, and she says, 'Thank you' and 'Merci,' because, like I said, she's in France."

The audience laughed.

Tater barked. Repeatedly. Abby nodded and stared at

the puppy as if she was picking up some sort of mental message.

"Tater says that if it weren't for you guys at the Coastal Animal Shelter, he never would've found a home with us and the millions of fans who invite *Dog Squad* into *their* homes all around the globe."

"It's true!" Tater said to an adoptable corgi named Meatball. "I said all that. Abby's a pet psychic!"

"Ha!" scoffed Meatball. "Says who?"

"Me! Abby's the real deal. We do mental telepathy together all the time."

"Sure you do, kid," said Meatball, waddling off with his handler. "Sure you do."

Abby went on to discuss how the Second Chance Ranch would be working with the Coastal Animal Shelter to help find homes for all the puppies who'd been stranded by Hurricane Adelaide.

When she said it, all the very well dressed ladies and gentlemen in the audience applauded heartily.

All except one.

The extremely wealthy Miss Kitty Bitteridge, who was seated at a table near the back of the tent.

She was only pretending to smile.

KITTY BITTERIDGE WAS having a horrible time at the charity gala.

The billionaire's sprawling estate bumped right up against the Second Chance Ranch's property. Yes, they were "next-door" neighbors, but the Bitteridge family had lived in Connecticut far longer than Jenny and Abby.

The Bitteridges were also far wealthier and far more important.

And yet, no one had ever thought to give Kitty Bitteridge a Pawscar Award at an over-the-top charity event in a circus-sized wedding tent! No one!

Because, as Miss Bitteridge knew all too well, there were too many dog people on the board of the Coastal Animal Shelter. She hated dog people. Oh yes, she knew that America was a dog country. But Kitty didn't care. She was a cat person. Why? Mostly because they reminded her of herself.

Elegant. Sophisticated. Aloof. Clever. And cunning!

If this were Switzerland, Austria, or Turkey, where cats outnumbered dogs three to one, Kitty Bitteridge would be the hero receiving all the accolades, not the foolish dog-trick trainers up the road at the Second Chance Ranch. Why, if Kitty had her way, no one would give that ranch a second glance. They'd learn that cats were far superior to dogs.

And soon, she *would* have her way.

Dimitri Kuznetsov, her chauffeur, would help. Dimitri had a head full of curls, a bushy walrus mustache, and a tuxedo, complete with a ruffled shirt, that had last been in fashion sometime in the early 1970s.

But he also had a very interesting history.

Before coming to America, Dimitri had worked as a cat trainer for a circus in Moscow. After a few unfortunate incidents under the big top (including one in front of the Russian president's terrified daughters), he was declared a Person of Much Disgrace and was asked, in no uncertain terms, to leave Russia and to take his flaming hoops with him.

"Next year, that statuette shall be mine," Kitty Bitter-idge whispered through gritted teeth.

Dimitri nodded. "Is next year when you will buy this statuette from your neighbor?"

"No, you fool. Next year, these dog-loving dunder-heads will award that Pawscar trophy to the one animal trainer who truly deserves it. Me, Dimitri! ME!"

SEAL TEAM SEVEN
EPISODE 5
OPENING SEQUENCE

SEVEN SEALS, ALL wearing tactical gear, leap off a rubber raft near a jagged ice floe somewhere in the Arctic Ocean.

They sluice through the water with tremendous strength, speed, and agility. Their whiskers twitch as they come upon a pair of divers activating the timer on an underwater bomb!

"Look, Kevin!" shrieks a wide-eyed seal. "It's Barnacle Bill and Seaweed Steve! They're going to blow up the North Pole!"

"They're trying to wipe out Christmas!" roars the crusty seal known as Sarge. "I hate when people try to do that!"

"Well, that's not gonna happen," says Kevin, Seal Team Seven's fearless and steely-eyed leader. "Team? It's time to seal the deal. Flex your flippers to the max!"

The seals kick into overdrive. Five team members swim and swirl and swoosh around the ticking bomb. Sarge and Bugeyes chase after the dastardly divers.

Meanwhile, back at the bomb, Tessa the tech seal studies the detonator. "There's no way to shut this thing down, boss!"

"Clear the area," Kevin tells his teammates. "It's snout time!"

The other seals do a quick backstroke away from the explosive device. Kevin dives deep, kicks his flippers, shoots up, and bops the mine with his nose as if it were a beach ball. The bomb sails out of the Arctic Ocean, climbs skyward, and explodes in the frigid air over a jagged glacier.

During this amazing action sequence, a hearty choir sings the *Seal Team Seven* theme song:

Seal Team Seven, *starring Kevin!*
They're slippery, slobbery, and sleek!
Seal Team Seven, *starring Kevin!*
Can they save the world . . . this week?

An announcer talks over the scrolling credits.

"America's favorite aquatic animal action-adventure series, *Seal Team Seven,* starring Kevin, the hero who gets everybody's seal of approval, will be right back!"

SMACK

BOOM

THE DOGS STILL at the Second Chance Ranch with Abby gathered in the big kennel to watch *Seal Team Seven* on a giant flat-screen TV—the same TV they watched whenever *Dog Squad* aired a new episode.

Dozer, a tough bulldog with a muscular chest, slammed down his front paw on the TV remote to change the channel.

"Forget them seals," he grumbled. "I'd rather watch *our* network!"

A slick promotion filled the screen. It showed all sorts of cats, dogs, horses, birds, turtles, and gerbils doing all sorts of incredible tricks.

"*America's Most Amazingly Talented Animals* is accepting audition clips for its new season. Win, and you'll go home with one million dollars!"

"Can you kindly paw the channel back to *Seal Team*

Seven?" sniffed Cha-Cha, the snooty chow chow who'd tried so hard to make sure Fred was a flop when he took over for the original Duke in *Dog Squad*.

"No," said Dozer, stomping on the remote to turn off the TV. "I can't believe that ridiculous walrus show is why me and Petunia ain't gonna get to do *Canine Commandos* no more."

"It's a very popular program," said Cha-Cha. "Last week, more people watched *Seal Team Seven* than watched *Dog Squad*."

"*Dog Squad* streamed a rerun last week," growled Petunia, the Doberman pinscher who'd been Dozer's best friend ever since they first met near a dumpster scrounging for scraps. "Reruns don't count!"

Cha-Cha shrugged. "I'm just saying. Don't be surprised when *Dog Squad* gets canceled just like *Canine Commandos* did."

"We didn't get canceled," grumbled Dozer. "We never got started!"

More dogs growled at Cha-Cha. She couldn't care less. She had a better fur coat than any of them.

"Knock it off, you mangy mongrels!" boomed a commanding voice.

It was Duke. The real Duke. The star who'd made *Dog Squad* a number one hit all around the globe before Fred took over.

"Hello, Duke," said Cha-Cha, her voice smoother than peanut butter without chunks. "How can we be of assistance to you today?"

"I wanted you mutts to know that I'm getting out while the getting's good. The vet just cleared me. I'm all better. I'm flying to Hollywood to live with Ella Olivia Posner."

All the dogs, even Dozer and Petunia, gasped.

"The YouTube star?" said a sad-eyed basset hound named Henry.

"That's right," said Duke. "Me and Ella are old pals. Ever since we costarred in that episode in season two. The one where I had to defuse a bomb with my teeth."

"Oh, that was a good one!" said Henry.

"They were all good when I was in 'em!" boasted Duke. "Now?" He shook his head. "Jenny made a huge mistake when she picked a chump to replace a champ."

And, of course, that was when Fred, Nala, and Scruffy scampered into the kennel.

"Hi, guys," said Fred.

"We're back from Paris," announced Nala.

"The one in France," added Scruffy. "Not Texas."

Fred wagged his tail eagerly. "How are things here?"

"Never better," sneered Duke. "I'm flying, first class, to Hollywood to live with Ella Olivia Posner! She has three swimming pools."

Nala whistled. She was impressed.

"Ella Olivia Posner?" said Scruffy. "Oh, she was good on the show."

"Better than you or Nala," sniffed Duke. "Anyway, good luck, everybody. Even though your fate may already be . . . *seal*ed! Those seals from *Seal Team Seven* are going to crush you and shut down your show. Who knows? In a couple of months, all of you might be moving to new homes too!"

FRED SAID MORE goodbyes the following week.

Nala was off to her goat yoga retreat.

Scruffy was leaving too.

"Mr. Espinosa is here, talking to Jenny. When they're done, I'm heading to Brooklyn, baby. They have locally sourced, artisanal dog food!"

"Wow!" said Fred. "What's that?"

"I dunno," said Scruffy. "But it tastes good. Plus, whenever Mr. Espinosa has pizza, he lets me eat the crusts."

Later, Fred felt a little lonely, sitting by himself on the porch of his designer doghouse—the beautiful bungalow that used to belong to the original Duke before he flew off to Hollywood. Would it ever really be Fred's? It felt so Duke-ish. It smelled Duke-ish too.

Fred was about to start feeling sorry for himself when Tater came bounding across the open lawn.

"Hiya, Fred!" Tater panted as he trundled up the steps to the porch. "I've got big news! BIG, big news!"

"Catch your breath first."

"Nope. I can't tell you the big news if I'm wasting time catching my breath. Besides, I'd rather catch a ball. Or a Frisbee. Or maybe a bumblebee."

"Okay, okay," Fred laughed. "What's going on?"

"You and me?" said Tater. "We're gonna star together in a brand-new show!"

"We are?" said Fred, arching an eyebrow. If true, this *would* be big news. In the kennels, all the dogs were talking about were shows that weren't being done (*Canine*

Commandos) or those in danger of being canceled (*Dog Squad*). How could there be a *new* show?

"I heard Jenny talking to Mr. Espinosa," said Tater. "They're worried about that other show, *Seal Team Seven*. It's stealing our audience."

Fred nodded. "So I've heard."

"Isn't stealing illegal?"

"Not in show business."

"Oh. Well, Mr. Espinosa says we have to do something new. Something bold. Something fresh! So guess what they're gonna do? Go on, Fred, guess!"

"A show with dolphins and porpoises?"

"Nope. They're gonna do *Cat Crew*!"

"Huh?"

"It's a crossover event! You and me, Fred. We'll be the only dogs from *Dog Squad* in it. And we'll help a crew of cats. That's why they call it *Cat Crew*."

"Aren't cats extremely difficult to train?" said Fred.

"Not if they're doing things they like to do. That's what Jenny says. And she's the best animal trainer I've ever met. She's also the only animal trainer I've ever met, but still . . ."

"When do we start?"

"A-S-A-P is what Mr. Espinosa said. I'm not sure what word he was spelling."

"As soon as possible," said Fred.

"Really? Four letters spell all those words? Wow."

Fred realized that if he was doing a new show, he

wouldn't be getting much of a break during his hiatus. But it was another way to say thank you to Jenny for rescuing him and giving him and so many other animals their home. The Second Chance Ranch was Fred's family now. But if shows kept getting canceled, maybe the family would have to split up. Like it did when Fred's Broadway show closed and he had to say goodbye to all his theater pals.

Clarence—the orange tabby who had played a bit part in an episode of *Dog Squad* with Fred—strolled past the porch, looking for the perfect spot to sun himself.

"Hey, Clarence!" shouted Tater. "You wanna hear some big news?"

"No thank you."

Tater kept going. "We're gonna do a new show. You and me and Fred!"

"We are?" said Clarence, stretching into a bored yawn.

"Yeah. It's gonna be called *Cat Crew.* And since you're a cat, you can be in it!"

"Oh, joy."

Clarence flopped on the ground and rolled around in some clover.

Uh-oh, thought Fred. *If a cat isn't excited about a new show starring cats, will anybody else be?*

9

"GUESS WE'LL BOTH be working over the break," Scruffy said to Fred as they watched Mr. Espinosa load Scruffy's things into the back of his compact SUV. "I'm gonna help Mr. Espinosa write you some good *Cat Crew* scripts."

"You are?"

"Oh yeah. He does his best writing on our walks. I think I give him ideas. Although, to be honest, I don't know much about cats."

"Me neither," said Fred.

Scruffy shrugged. "What's to know? Other than that cats have been our mortal enemies since time immemorial."

"Huh?"

"Means we dogs have been hating cats for so long, nobody knows when, how, or why it got started."

"I don't *hate* cats," said Fred. "I've never really known any. I mean, sure, there's Clarence. And when I was down in New York City, there was this one cat named Mehitabel. She lived in the alley. I never actually met her, though. . . ."

"So how'd you know her name?"

"She used to yowl it at the moon all night long. 'I'm Mehitabel! I'm ME-HIT-A-BEL!' It went on and on for hours."

Mr. Espinosa closed the hatchback on his vehicle.

"Oh boy," said Scruffy. "Here it comes. Wait for it. Wait for it. . . ."

Mr. Espinosa turned around, whistled twice, and slapped both his hands against his thighs.

"Come on, Scruffy. Time to go. It's pizza night!"

"That's my cue, Freddy boy. Have fun with all the kitty cats!"

He was off like a shot and leapt into the backseat of the car.

Fred's tail drooped as Mr. Espinosa's tires crunched up the pebbly driveway. His two best friends, Nala and Scruffy, had both left the ranch.

They got a real "hiatus."

Fred got to work with cats.

"There you are!" said Abby, coming down from the house. Tater trailed behind her.

"I told Abby where to find you," said Tater. "We did some more of that mind-reading pet-psychic stuff we do."

Fred nodded. He actually (well, kind of, sort of) believed that Tater and Abby had a telepathic connection.

One time, during a very dangerous situation, Tater had communicated through Abby to tell Fred what to do.

"Come on, Fred," said Abby. "We're going to the cat cottage."

She led the way across an open field.

"Aunt Jenny thinks it'd be a good idea for you guys to spend a little time getting to know the cats we already have. There's Clarence, Mister Cookiepants, and Barney. Barney used to be a barn cat. Of course, Mr. Espinosa wants six or seven cats in the cast, so Aunt Jenny's contacting all the animal shelters in the area, looking for more. Mr. Espinosa says the Cat Crew has to look different from the Dog Squad."

"Well, it will!" yipped Tater. "They'll be cats."

"Riiiiight," said Fred.

This whole idea was sounding shakier and shakier. Like something Jenny and Mr. Espinosa were throwing together the way they might scramble dinner scraps in a dog food bowl. Because of *Seal Team Seven*. Duke was probably right. Those seals were going to crush Fred, *Dog Squad,* and all the good being done at the Second Chance Ranch.

Unless . . .

Unless Fred could figure out a way to make this goofy idea about cats and dogs fighting crime (instead of each other) work.

"Go on in, you guys!" said Abby. "I'll wait for you out here. Take your time."

Fred and Tater stepped into the cat cottage and got a good, strong whiff of cat. It might've been cat pee. Or cat poop. Or just CAT.

"P.U.," Fred whispered to Tater. "Something sure stinks in here."

"You're right," huffed a puffy gray cat with a squished-in face. He was sitting in a very gymnastic pose on his back haunches so he could lick his belly fur. "It's you two! You both smell like dogs!"

"UH, HI," SAID Fred, trying his best to cover up for his rude remark, which the cats really weren't supposed to hear. "Mmm. Like I said, something sure smells delicious. Is that fish? Shrimp? Catnip?"

"No," said the cat. "As I stated earlier, it is you two. There's no more offensive, foul, nor odiferous scent in the world than dog. Except, of course, *wet* dog."

"You tell them, Mister Cookiepants," said Clarence, sounding even more bored than usual. He was lounging on a carpeted cat tree, basking in the warmth of a sunbeam.

"Woo-eee," said the disheveled mass of fur who had to be Barney the barn cat. "I'll tell you what. Them two dogs down there smell so bad, if they was playin' in a sandbox, I'd have to bury 'em."

Tater giggled. "You guys are funny! We're gonna make a funny TV show together."

"Oh, really? Says who?" inquired Mister Cookiepants.

"Jenny!" said Tater. "And Abby. And Mr. Espinosa."

"Sure it's a wacky idea," said Fred. "But we all have to work together."

Mister Cookiepants sniffed haughtily. "We are cats. We do not work well with others, for we, unlike you, are not pack animals. Besides, we only do that which we want to do. We will not automatically sit or give you our paw or, heaven forbid, 'roll over' simply because you offer us a freeze-dried salmon treat."

"We only do those things if and when we feel like it," added Clarence.

"But you still gotta give us the dad-burned salmon treat," said Barney.

"You guys?" said Tater. "This is super important."

"That's where you are wrong," said Mister Cookiepants. "Nothing is important in this world except breakfast, lunch, and dinner."

Fred didn't know what to do. He looked toward the door.

Maybe Abby could pull him and Tater out of this awkward situation.

But Abby was gone.

She had drifted up the hill to chat with Zachary Babkow, a boy her own age. Zachary's father, Mr. Babkow, was the ranch's handyman. Zachary came by from time to time to help his father and, if Fred was reading things correctly, to spend time with Abby.

They could talk about everything and nothing for a long, long, long time. Abby wouldn't be coming back for Fred and Tater anytime soon.

"Look," said Fred, "I know you guys aren't excited about working with dogs . . ."

"Ha!" said Mister Cookiepants.

"Why don't you two hightail it on outta here?" suggested Barney. "You're barkin' up the wrong tree. Y'all are our sworn enemies."

Fred was frustrated.

First of all, he hadn't been barking. Second of all, the cats were the ones up the carpeted trees. And third of all—

"Yo! Fred!"

Dozer, the slobbering bulldog, waddled into the cat cottage.

"Ewwww! Gross!" whined all three cats.

"This one doesn't just stink," gasped Mister Cookiepants. "It has stringy droolcicles dangling off its lips!"

"Deal with it, fish breath," Dozer snarled. He turned to Fred. "I been lookin' everywheres for you."

"What's wrong?"

"I'm pickin' up a distress signal from Petunia."

"Where is she?"

"On patrol. Prowling along the fence separating our ranch from that swanky mansion next door. She needs backup. And my legs are too stubby to dash over to see what all the fuss is about. But I gotta tell ya, pal—it sure sounds like some kind of trouble."

Fred perked up.

Dozer had just given him a great excuse for fleeing the cat cottage.

"Well, Dozer," Fred said in his most dramatic Duke voice, "when trouble calls, it's Dog Squad to the rescue."

"Only, right now, you're not really a squad, Fred," Tater peeped. "You're just one dog."

"Don't matter," said Dozer. "Petunia needs help!"

"And sometimes," said Fred, cocking his head just so to feel even more Duke-ish, "one dog is all it takes. Dozer? Keep an eye on Tater. So long, feline friends. We'll continue this discussion when I don't have urgent business to attend to."

Fred dashed out the door.

"We ain't your dadgum friends!" he heard Barney yowling behind him.

But he couldn't let that distract him. He had to hurry.

He had to find Petunia.

He had to stop smelling cat pee.

FRED FLAPPED UP his ears and focused.

There!

He heard Petunia's bark. It was faint, but its meaning was clear: "Help!"

Fred kicked himself into overdrive and ran even faster. His heart pounded. His breathing was hard and heavy. He scooted through a thick stand of trees and raced into an open meadow.

He saw Charlie the horse grazing on a patch of grass near the white plank fencing. From what Nala had told Fred, Charlie had once worked in a circus. Now he was old and gray and nearly blind. Jenny had given Charlie a stable in a barn where he could live out his final years with grace and dignity.

"Hey, Fred!" Petunia cried. "Over here. This is an emergency-type situation!"

Petunia was farther down the fence line. She was

standing guard beneath a massive oak tree. Its trunk straddled the boundary between the Second Chance Ranch and the sprawling estate on the other side.

Fred skidded to a stop beside Petunia.

"What's up?" Fred asked, the way Duke would in an episode of *Dog Squad*.

"That darn cat!" said Petunia, nudging her snout skyward.

Fred saw a terrified kitten. Its eyes were as wide as coat buttons.

It was meowing pitifully.

Because it was stuck in the tree.

"Help me," the little kitten peeped sadly. "Help me. Please?"

Petunia shook her head. "Cats, they can climb up, but they can't climb down. Am I right?"

"Yes," said Fred.

He looked up at the kitten. It made him feel dizzy. The branch wasn't as high up as the Eiffel Tower, but still . . .

"Unfortunately," he said, shaking his head to get rid of the vertigo, "we dogs can't climb up *or* down a tree. All we can do is leap."

Which Fred tried.

He slammed himself against the oak tree's nubby bark.

"Youch," said Petunia.

Fred shook out his fur, pulled himself together, and tried again. This time, he gave himself a longer head start.

He sprinted across the grassy field.

He leapt.

He splayed open his limbs.

He crashed into the tree.

And knocked all the wind out of his chest. Again.

"That'll sting," said Petunia.

Fred grimaced. "Hang in there, little fella," he grunted up to the kitten.

"I am, I am," squeaked the kitten.

"Where'd you come from?" Fred asked.

The kitten gasped in fear. "Why?"

"Your people must be worried."

"No! They're horrible! Don't make me go back! No! Please!"

"Whoa," said Fred. "Let's take this one step at a time. First we need to get you out of this predicament."

"It's not a predicament! It's a tree!"

"Excuse me, friends," said a deep voice.

Fred and Petunia both turned around. Charlie the horse had loped over to join them.

"HIYA, CHARLIE!" SAID Fred, wagging his tail and smiling up at the noble horse.

"Hiya," said Charlie with a friendly flick of his mane. "What brings you to my pasture, Fred, or should I call you Duke?"

"Fred is fine. I'm off duty."

"There's a cat up this tree," said Petunia.

"So I gathered," said Charlie with a slow nod. "Cats are great climbers. A skill that allows them to quickly escape danger."

"But how do cats scamper *down* a tree?" asked Fred.

"Well, that's the problem. Their curved claws work extremely well to grasp onto the bark as they clamber *up*. However, those same claws were not designed to help them climb down. To descend a tree, a cat must scoot backward."

"Wow," whistled Petunia. "For a horse, you sure know a lot about cats."

The horse laughed. "I used to work with some very clever cats back in my circus days."

"Did you ever have a cat up a tree in your circus act?" asked Fred.

"No," said the horse. "But we did have this one frisky scamp who loved to make high dives onto my back."

At the mere mention of high dives, Fred's stomach did a backflip.

"Rascal was his name," Charlie continued. "He'd scrabble up a skinny ladder to a diving board thirty feet above the ring.

The snare drum would roll. The crowd would gasp. And that daredevil cat would slink his way out to the edge of that perch."

"And then what happened?" asked Petunia.

"The lady in the spangly leotard made certain I was positioned just so, right underneath Rascal. I'd give him my secret whinny. He'd jump and land on my back."

"So, what's the secret whinny?" asked Fred.

"Oh, any whinny will do. Cats understand what they mean."

"What's a whinny?" asked Petunia.

"A friendly, high-pitched neigh," said Charlie. "It's how we horses find each other, especially when we're feeling lonely. Cats hear that friendliness in your voice, they'll leap into action, lickety-split."

And with that, the horse held up his head, flapped open his mouth, and, lips quivering around his huge teeth, let loose with a loud "Nee-eee-eee-eee-ha!"

The kitten sprang out of the tree. It shot out all four legs, shrieked "Yippeeeeee," tucked in its paws, and made a perfect, soft four-point landing!

"THANKS, MR. HORSE!" the kitten mewed. "That was fun!"

"You're welcome," said Charlie. "I had fun too. Felt like old times!"

"That was amazing," said Fred. "You're very good with cats."

Charlie chuckled. "I guess I am. And, Fred? You will be too."

"Huh?"

"Oh, I hear things. Everybody's talking about how you're going to star in a brand-new show called *Cat Crew*."

"Well," said Fred, "that's Jenny's plan."

"Sounds like a good one to me. Just make sure you and the cats are having fun. Go on. Give this kitten a whinny."

"Um, I'm not a horse. So . . ."

"Use your voice. Let her know you're a friend looking for a friend."

Fred thought about that.

No way could he whinny like Charlie.

But . . .

He did have a certain playful whimper he sometimes used when he was meeting a dog for the first time and wanted to let that other dog know he meant no harm. That he just wanted to wrestle or roughhouse for fun.

He offered up an inviting, lilting whine.

When the kitten heard it, her ears shot up and her head tilted sideways.

"Hello, friend!" she squeaked down to Fred.

She hopped off Charlie's back and landed on Fred with a soft thud.

"Well, look at that," remarked Petunia. "The kitty cat wants to ride *you* instead of the horse!"

Fred puffed up his chest and tried to look as dignified and noble as he could with a kitten holding on to his head.

"Hang on to my ears," he said. "Let's go introduce you to Jenny. Who knows? If things work out, you might be starring with me in *Cat Crew*!"

"KITTEN NUMBER NINE is missing!" Dimitri Kuznetsov told Kitty Bitteridge.

Miss Bitteridge hissed and clawed at the air with her leopard-print gloves to let Dimitri know how very displeased she was with this news.

"What about the other eight kittens?" she asked.

"Da," Dimitri replied in his thick accent. "They are fine. They are all in their kitten cubicles, learning the basics. Becoming accustomed to . . ."

He paused for dramatic effect.

". . . the collar!"

A bright smile blossomed on Miss Bitteridge's cherry-red lips.

"Good, Dimitri. Good. The collar is their friend."

"Da," said the famous (but disgraced) Russian animal trainer.

Miss Bitteridge marched across her basement gymnasium's floor to where ten purebred Abyssinian cats stood stock-still in a tight formation. Each one was facing a small hoop and a balance beam.

"Forget the kittens for now, Dimitri. To win *America's Most Amazingly Talented Animals,* we must focus on our Abyssinian drill team!"

Abyssinians were considered the smartest cat breed of all. Each Abyssinian was wearing a special collar that had been designed by Dimitri and some renegade electronics engineers. All ten cats were ready to do whatever Miss Bitteridge commanded them to do. They would soon show the world that cats could perform tricks and stunts as well as dogs. No, they could do it better. Why, these nimble and acrobatic athletes would one day rival the Radio City Rockettes!

Miss Bitteridge twiddled her gloved fingers. The ten cats leapt through ten hoops in perfect synchronicity.

Miss Bitteridge wiggled a different finger sequence.

The cats hopped onto their highly polished balance beams and stepped forward, placing one padded paw in front of the other. They reached the end of their narrow planks at the exact same second, planted their front paws, and raised their hindquarters—awaiting their next command.

Miss Bitteridge tapped the tip of her second finger against her thumb.

The cats executed a perfect double-somersault back-flip off their beams and nailed a perfect landing on the padded mat.

Well, nine of them did.

The newest one did not.

"Dimitri?" said Miss Bitteridge, arching an eyebrow.

"That is Number Ten. The Abyssinian I recruited from the alley in New York City. He's only been collared for two days. He will soon catch up with the others."

"I'm sure he will," said Miss Bitteridge with a malevolent smile. She squeezed the pinky finger on her left hand. It was, of course, her tenth digit.

The newest cat screeched.

The electric shock collar always made them screech.

"Let's try it one more time," boomed Miss Bitteridge. "Now!"

The ten cats scurried back to their starting positions facing the ten hoops.

They were ready to rehearse the routine again.

And again.

And again.

None of them wanted to feel the tingling jolt that would zap them the instant they made a mistake!

THE CATS AND TRAINERS in the sprawling mansion's basement gymnasium didn't see the two mangy alley cats watching their every move.

Mehitabel and Yakster were hunkered down in the shrubbery outside a casement window. They peered into the cellar and studied the training exercises.

"Oh boy," whispered Yakster, a chatty Siamese mix. "What have they done to Einstein? He looks like he's been brainwashed. I don't even like to have my ears washed! What are we gonna do, Mehitabel?"

Mehitabel was a black cat with a white patch on her chest. She was clever, crafty, and somewhat mysterious. She called herself a "wise old soul," claiming to have lived many, many lives. More than a typical cat's nine.

"Well, my friend," she said to Yakster, "we must find a way to free Einstein from his captors!"

"It's impossible. We can't do it. Not on our own. No way. No can do."

Mehitabel sighed. "You could be correct. We might need to seek assistance."

Only a few days earlier, the two shabby cats perched near the window had been alley cats in New York City. Einstein, the Abyssinian, had been a loyal member of their crew. Together, the three cats made nightly forays into the treasures of the darkened alley's trash bins. They shared whatever they scrounged with less fortunate felines. Einstein always knew where to hunt for food. In fact, he had saved several homeless cats from certain starvation.

"Einstein was so smart," said Yakster. "A real brainiac. There wasn't a dumpster he couldn't crack. Now? He looks like a zombie!"

Mehitabel placed a comforting paw on Yakster's shoulder. "Do not despair, my friend. Once we complete our rescue mission, we shall return to all the gourmet garbage the city and its finer alleyways have to offer."

"But wait a second," said Yakster. "How are we gonna make it all the way back to New York City? It's not like we can hitch another ride with the evil Russian cat snatcher unless he goes rushin' back to the city to snatch another cat, which maybe he'll do because he's evil. But we can't count on it."

When the Russian man had snatched Einstein out of the alley, Mehitabel and Yakster had chased after his pickup truck. They had leapt up into its cargo bed and ridden through the night with their caged comrade as he was whisked off to his fate north of the city in the wooded wilds of a land called Connecticut.

"I blame myself for Einstein's capture," said Mehitabel. "A pizza topped with anchovies just sitting there inside a metal crate? I should've been more suspicious. In retrospect, it reminds me of the clever booby traps set by my former owner, the Red Queen of Palenque, who ruled the Maya empire in AD 650."

Yakster nodded. He was used to Mehitabel's tales of her past lives.

But this story was cut short by a chorus of angry hisses and screeches.

Down below, the zombie cats in the basement were staring up at the window.

All ten, including Einstein, were pointing their paws as if they were hunting dogs.

Now the man and the woman looked up at the window.

"Who are these spies?" snarled the Russian cat snatcher.

"Nosy strays!" snapped the woman.

She twiddled her gloved fingertips. The Abyssinians spasmed in pain.

"Sic them!" shouted the woman.

The Abyssinians marched single file toward a staircase.

"Double time!" shouted the woman, wiggling her fingers faster.

The cats twitched and picked up their pace.

Mehitabel and Yakster gave each other a panicked look.

And ran away from the window, fast!

16

"**THEY'RE GAINING ON** us!" shrieked Yakster. "We should split up. They can't chase both of us, can they? I guess they could. There's ten of 'em. Five could chase you, five could chase me."

"My friend," said Mehitabel without missing a stride,

"I am reminded of something a wise old lion named Mufasa told me that time I was a panther in Africa: If you want to go fast, go alone. If you want to go far, go together!"

"I'm for fast. Zippity-zip-zip, zoom!"

"But 'far' might be the safer option given our upcoming obstacle."

"You mean this river?"

Yakster and Mehitabel skidded to a stop on the bank of some swiftly moving water. A hundred yards behind them, across a wide swath of lawn, the ten Abyssinians were marching in lockstep, shrieking a terrifying war cry, and moving closer.

"Actually," yabbered Yakster, "it's not really a river. More of a stream. Or a creek. You could also call it a rivulet or a brook."

"Let's discuss our word choices later, shall we?"

Mehitabel sprang into a nearby willow tree and scurried up one of its long and supple limbs. Her weight, slight though it was, caused the bendable branch to dip across the narrow creek. As Mehitabel scampered along the flexible limb, its feathery leaves plunged deeper into the stream.

"Cross the Willow Bridge!" she called to Yakster.

"Okay, okay. I'll cross it."

Yakster scooted over the stream.

Just when both alley cats were safe, the army of glazed-eyed Abyssinians arrived on the far bank.

Mehitabel leapt off the branch.

It flipped back up like the firing arm of a catapult. Since the dunked leaves were soaked, they showered the attack cats with creek water. It was as if Mehitabel had just flicked a giant leafy paintbrush at her attackers.

The sprinkled Abyssinians hissed angrily.

Mehitabel made eye contact with Einstein. He looked like, maybe, he wanted to wave or call out.

But he was too terrified.

Mehitabel nodded slowly to let her friend know that everything would soon be okay. That they would not abandon him. That somehow, some way, she and Yakster would return to rescue their friend.

The sinister cat snatcher and the lady in the kitty-print dress finally arrived at the creek bank.

"Scat, you horrible creatures!" screamed the woman, shaking her gloved fist. "Your type isn't welcome here!"

"You do not belong on this property!" shouted the man. "You are far too ordinary for Miss Kitty Bitteridge's championship show team!"

The lady with the ruby-red lips fidgeted her fingers.

The ten cats raised their heads and tails to strike a rigid pose. The lady tapped her pinky to her thumb, and they all pivoted into a 180-degree turn in perfect synchronicity.

Einstein was playing along. Making all the stilted moves. Blending in with the cultish cat crowd.

"Fear not, Einstein!" Mehitabel cried out. "We shall return. You will not be forgotten. This I promise."

Mehitabel could see Einstein give a quick flutter of his tail in reply as he marched with the others back to the mansion.

"So, boss, how are we gonna rescue, Einstein?" asked Yakster. "By the way, he doesn't look so good. In fact, he looks bad. Awful, really."

Mehitabel was only half listening.

She was scoping out her surroundings. Contemplating her next moves.

"We need a safe place to regroup and plot our rescue mission," she told Yakster.

"Safe sounds good. Like we'd be out of danger."

The two alley cats hiked uphill, away from the creek.

They traipsed through a densely forested area until they came to a white plank fence penning in a meadow. There was a cozy barn at one end of the field.

"Aha! That shall be our new headquarters, Yakster," said Mehitabel. "We will rest there and strategize. And when the time is ripe, we will once more cross that rippling creek and free Einstein!"

FRED AND TATER were amazed as they watched Jenny work with the kitten in the cat cottage.

Work really wasn't the right word. It was more like they were playing and the kitten was having so much fun she didn't realize she was learning tricks.

"Again, again!" the kitten peeped every time Jenny gave her a small chunk of chicken as a reward for doing what Jenny had asked. Instead of meowing, the kitten chirped and squeaked with glee.

"We should call her Chirp," said Fred.

"Or Squeak!" said Tater.

"Hey, Aunt Jenny?" said Abby.

"Yes, hon?" said Jenny, who had already taught the kitten how to slap a high five with her paw.

"We should name the kitten Squeak."

"Oh. That's a good name for her."

"Yeah. Tater came up with it."

Jenny arched one skeptical eyebrow. Fred could tell: Jenny still wasn't completely sold on her niece's pet-psychic mind-reading abilities.

"Before we give her a name," said Jenny, "we should take her to the vet. See if she's microchipped. She looks to be a purebred Abyssinian. I wouldn't be surprised if she already has a home . . . maybe a name, too."

"No!" peeped Squeak. "It's not a home. It's a prison!"

Fred and Tater both nodded. They understood what the kitten was squealing about in her high-pitched screech. All Jenny and Abby heard was "SQUEAK-SQUEAK-SQUEAKITY-PEEP-SQUEAK."

That was probably why Jenny laughed. "But you're right, Tater," she said, giving the puppy a good ear scratch. "Squeak would be the perfect name for her. If she doesn't already have a different one."

"Kitten Number Nine!" yelped the kitten. "That was my name. Don't make me go back! Please, please, please, please, please!"

This last outburst came out as a series of ear-piercing screeches.

"Come on, Abby. Let's get 'Squeak' into a carrier. We'll go see Beth."

"Dr. Appleman?"

Jenny nodded. "She can do a scan for the ID chip and give this kitten a checkup."

"If she doesn't have a microchip," said Abby eagerly, "can we keep her, Aunt Jenny? Squeak's such a fast learner. She'd be great in *Cat Crew*!"

Jenny smiled. "We'll see, Abby."

As they eased the kitten into a soft-sided cat bag with mesh windows, Zachary Babkow came into the cat cottage lugging two fluffy dog beds. One was big, the other puppy-sized.

Zachary smiled at Abby. Abby smiled at Zachary.

Fred wagged his tail happily.

"What?" said Tater. "What's going on?"

Fred chuckled. "Nothing."

"Then why are you chuckling?"

"Yeah," cheeped Squeak.

Fred ignored them both. They were too young to understand mushy stuff.

"Where do you want these, Ms. Yen?" Zachary asked.

"How about that corner? Fred likes to sleep in a corner."

Jenny had Squeak's cat bag slung over one shoulder. She bent down to have a word with Fred and Tater.

"I want you two to really get to know your *Cat Crew* castmates, so you'll be sleeping in here for a while."

"Oh boy," panted Tater. "An adventure in Catland! It's like we're visiting a different country where we don't know the language and everybody eats stinky food we won't like."

"Have fun," said Jenny, patting Fred on the head. "We start work on *Cat Crew* first thing tomorrow morning."

Fred gave Jenny a nervous smile and the best tail wag he could muster. He wanted her to know he'd do anything to help. He'd give this whole cat-immersion thing his best shot.

Even if they did smell funny.

CLARENCE, BARNEY, AND Mister Cookiepants had been catnapping in the cottage the whole time Jenny had been training Squeak.

Now they stretched themselves awake.

"Mmmmm," said Barney. "Somethin' sure smells finer than a frog hair split four ways."

"That's chicken!" said Tater. "Jenny had chicken!"

"Ahhh," said Mister Cookiepants, savoring the lingering aroma. "No wonder I was having the most deliciously delightful dream. I dreamt I lived with Colonel Sanders. He graciously gave me free samples of his Kentucky Fried Chicken. It was yummy."

"Jenny was training Squeak!" said Tater enthusiastically, which was how he said everything. "She was using chicken as a reward."

"Jenny always gives us a treat when we do what she asks us to do for *Dog Squad*," added Fred.

"Because," said Clarence, "you are dogs. You will do anything, no matter how humiliating, for a treat."

"Jenny never makes us do anything humiliating or dangerous," said Fred.

"But you'd do it if'n she wanted you to," said Barney. "If'n Jenny dangled a li'l ol' liver snap underneath your snout."

"We, on the other hand, are more . . . finicky," said Mister Cookiepants. "We will not debase ourselves for table scraps."

"But," said Tater, "we need you! We can't do *Cat Crew* without *cats*."

Clarence yawned. "I need another nap."

"Same here," said Barney.

"Capital idea," agreed Mister Cookiepants. "I want to get back to my dream. The Colonel promised me gravy."

The three cats curled up into furry balls and fell asleep.

Again.

For hours.

They could sleep all day.

Which, Fred discovered, meant they *didn't* sleep at night.

No. At night, they chased each other.

They played skittle pool with bottle caps, thwacking bank shots off the baseboards. They scampered. They pranced, they danced, and they cavorted.

"Tater?" Fred finally whispered.

The puppy was sound asleep. Probably because he exhausted himself every day.

Fred wished he could do the same. He had to get some sleep. Jenny said they were starting work on *Cat Crew* first thing in the morning. And, technically, it was already morning. Fred shuttered his eyelids.

But they sprang back open when Clarence pounced on a squeak toy.

Then Barney THWACKed another bottle cap.

Fred couldn't take it anymore. He had to get away from the cat chaos!

Yes, Jenny and Abby wanted him to "spend time" with the cats. But Fred needed to spend time SLEEPING! So he trotted out of the cottage and went home to his doghouse.

Ah! Quiet. Comfy. Perfect!

He'd barely closed his eyes when—

MEOW!

THWACK!

SQUEAK!

The noise and clatter from the cat cottage rolled across the open field, right into Fred's dog bed.

He needed to spend the night somewhere else. Somewhere quiet. Somewhere far away.

Of course, he thought. *Charlie's place!*

The old horse had that barn. Charlie didn't play games with bottle caps or squeeze squeak toys. Sure, sometimes he slept standing up, like horses do, but Fred could deal with that.

And so, while the three cats kept proving just how nocturnal they truly were, Fred once again trotted out into the night. He would bunk with Charlie.

He, of course, didn't know that Charlie already had sleepover guests.

Or that they were both wide awake too.

FRED PADDED ACROSS the dewy meadow, heading for Charlie's barn.

The night was quiet. Except for crickets and the croak of distant frogs. But as Fred approached the wooden structure, he thought he heard meowing. Purrs, too.

Argh! Those horrible noises are still ringing in my ears, he told himself. *It's the soundtrack to my nightmare, even though I'm wide awake.*

The meowing stopped the instant Fred stuck his head inside the barn's arched entryway. Charlie was standing stock-still in a stall, silhouetted in the moonlight.

"Hello? Charlie? It's me. Fred. Are you asleep?"

"No," said Charlie. "Not anymore."

"Sorry. Didn't mean to wake you. I need somewhere quiet to sleep tonight. My doghouse is too close to the cat cottage. They're very noisy. Especially at night."

"Well, you're welcome here. Just promise me you won't chase my other two guests."

Fred tilted his head slightly. "You have other guests?"

"I suspect he is referring to us," said a black cat with a white patch on her chest. She emerged from the inky shadows. "Allow me to introduce myself. I am Mehitabel."

"You're a cat," said Fred.

"How very observant of you, my friend."

"Much like you," Charlie explained in his smooth and mellow voice, "Mehitabel and her companion needed a safe haven. I told them all peaceful creatures are welcome here."

"And we're very peaceful," said a twitchy cat with big buggy eyes. He burped. Twice. "Charlie let us share his feed bag. Delish. We don't usually eat horse food. But beggars can't be choosers, even though choosers *can* be beggars but not very good ones because they're so choosy." He spoke so fast, the words blurred together.

"Forgive me for staring," said the black cat. "You look so familiar."

"Well, your *name* sounds familiar," said Fred. "Is it really Mehitabel?"

"Yes. I named myself after the cat Don Marquis wrote about in the early nineteen hundreds. I loved reading his Archy and Mehitabel stories in the newspaper when I lived with a hepcat jazz musician uptown in Harlem."

Fred nodded slowly. "You've been alive since the early nineteen hundreds?"

Mehitabel laughed. So did her friend.

"No," said the chatty cat. "That was during her, what, eighty-seventh life?"

"Actually," said Mehitabel, "it was my eighty-sixth."

"Did you, in any of your lives, ever live in New York City?" asked Fred. "In a place called Shinbone Alley?"

"Oh yes. In fact, when we're not on the road, Shinbone Alley is our home."

"Do you shout your name at the moon?"

"Only when it's full. Aha! I know where I've seen you. You star in *Dog Squad*."

Fred wagged his tail.

"Yeah. I'm Fred. I play Duke."

"Oh, you're good," said the Siamese. "There's an appliance store around the corner from our alley with all sorts of TVs in their windows. Nothin' better than dragging a half-eaten tuna fish sandwich out of the trash, settling down in the gutter, and watching a bunch of dogs do heroic stuff."

"Forgive me," said Mehitabel. "I should have made introductions. This is my dear friend Yakster. It seems you know our host, Charlie?"

"Sure. He helped me rescue a kitten out of a tree."

"Is that so?" said Mehitabel, slinking forward, her eyes inquisitive. "Didn't you also rescue a cat in a recent episode of your show?"

"Yep. That was Clarence. He's one of the cats here at the Second Chance Ranch. He might star with me in a new show called *Cat Crew*."

"And will there be more daring rescues and escapes in this new show?"

"Not sure," said Fred. "Jenny hasn't told us what we're going to do yet."

"But you like attempting rescues?"

Fred smiled eagerly. "Oh yeah. Rescues are the best. Especially if there's a helicopter in it. We've done water rescues. Top-secret spy mission rescues. Alligator pit rescues. Underwater— Hey, wait a minute. You guys are cats. I need a cat crew. And the cats bunking in the cat cottage just want to sleep all the time. How'd you like to be in the new show with me? You'd have to learn some tricks and stuff, but I promise it'll be fun. Who knows, we might even get to do another rescue scene."

"A rescue scene, you say?" Mehitabel grinned. "Why, that would be purr-fect. Absolutely purr-fect."

AN HOUR OR so later, Mehitabel crept over to where the dog named Fred was snoozing on a bale of hay.

Fred was also passing a little gas.

Mehitabel waved her paw under her nose to whisk away the odor.

"He's still asleep," she whispered to Yakster.

"He's still stinky, too," said Yakster.

"Indeed. But might I suggest we take this dog up on his offer? Participating in this *Cat Crew* production will enable us to gain valuable new skills. Skills of the sort we could utilize to rescue Einstein. Why, I remember my time with Abraham Lincoln at the White House. I was but one of several strays he took in, but we all learned a great deal during the war cabinet meetings we were privy to."

Mehitabel smiled, remembering her time with America's sixteenth president.

"I was a tabby when Honest Abe fed me with a golden

spoon at a state dinner. Mrs. Lincoln did not approve. Mr. Lincoln did not care. Good times."

Yakster nodded and waited for Mehitabel to drift back from another one of her past-life memories. She always had a far-off, glassy look in her eyes when she remembered one of the cats she'd been before.

"So," she said, snapping out of her trance, "we play along, Yakster. We learn what we can. We bide our time. And then, when the enemy least expects it, we strike!"

Yakster raised his paw.

"Yes?" said Mehitabel.

"Are the humans who trapped Einstein the enemy in this present-day scenario?"

"Yes," said Mehitabel. "For they broke up our happy family."

So, early the next morning, the two alley cats said their goodbyes to Charlie and followed Fred.

"This way," said Fred, wagging his white-tipped tail like a battle flag. "We're heading up to the cat cottage. That's where the cats live."

"Really?" said Mehitabel, trying very hard not to sound sarcastic. "My, what a simple yet descriptive name."

Suddenly, a small puppy came bounding down the hill.

"Woo-hoo! More cats for *Cat Crew*! Way to go, Fred. I wondered where you were! Out on a recruiting mission, huh? Hello, cats! Welcome, welcome, welcome!"

The small dog leapt up and bumbled into Yakster.

The two tumbled around on the ground. The puppy's tail was wagging. Yakster's was not.

Mehitabel heard very loud, very sloppy slurping sounds. Apparently the puppy was also licking or, perhaps, grooming the Siamese cat.

"Meet Tater," said Fred. "He's very excited to see you guys."

"I am, I am," said Tater. "And guess what? Jenny has our first script. It's a rescue scene!"

Mehitabel's eyes lit up. "Meow-velous!" she said. "Lead on, good sirs. Lead on."

"WELL, WHO HAVE we here?" asked Jenny when Fred and Tater proudly padded into the cottage, trailed by the two scruffy cats.

"They kind of look like alley cats," said Abby.

"Oh, they just need a good brushing," said Jenny.

"Fred found 'em!" said Tater.

"I think Fred found them," Abby said to her aunt.

"Is that so?" said Jenny.

"Yep. It sure is," said Tater. "He told me their names are Mehitabel and Yakster."

Abby relayed the names to her aunt Jenny.

"Uh-huh," said Jenny. "Did Tater tell you that, too?"

Abby nodded. "He got it from Fred."

"That's Jenny, our trainer," Fred told the new cats. "Abby is her niece. She's also an assistant trainer. Those three cats sound asleep in their cat beds? That's Clarence, Barney, and Mister Cookiepants."

"We can use these new strays in the show," said Abby. "If we added them to Squeak and the others, we'd have six cats. That's definitely enough for a crew!"

"Excuse me," Mehitabel said to Fred. "Did that young lady just call us strays?"

"Yeah," said Fred. "She didn't mean anything by it. . . ."

"We are not strays!" protested Yakster.

"Doesn't matter!" peeped a tiny voice.

A small kitten clambered up and over the edge of a soft cat bed.

"You two need to play nice, because these people are nice. Nicer than those monsters next door. They called me Kitten Number Nine. Now I'm Squeak!"

Fred noticed that Mehitabel was studying the kitten very closely.

"Pardon my staring, Squeak," said Mehitabel, "but you appear to be an Abyssinian."

"That's right."

"Were you by any chance a member of—"

The kitten covered her ears with her front paws. "Brrr-ring, brrr-ring, brrr-ring. I am not listening to you. . . ."

Mehitabel gave Squeak a reassuring look. "I understand. We shall discuss this at a more convenient time."

Jenny bent down to smile at the new cats.

"Welcome to the Second Chance Ranch, Mehitabel and Yakster."

Each of the cats nodded when Jenny spoke their name.

"You're both welcome to stay here at the ranch. And, if you want, you can play with us too. I'll teach you a few tricks. But only tricks you want to do . . ."

The kitten went up on her haunches and slapped her paw against Jenny's open palm.

"That's called a high five," the kitten Squeak reported. "I learned it yesterday."

"Way to go!" said Tater, raising his paw to slap pads with Squeak.

"We'll need to run these two by Dr. Appleman," Jenny told Abby. "Have them scanned for microchips, like we did with Squeak."

"I could take their pictures and make up some Missing Cat posters," suggested Abby.

"That might be a good idea. Let me call Beth. See when she can fit us in."

Jenny stepped outside to make the phone call.

Mehitabel turned to Tater. "No Missing Cat posters. We need to avoid certain nefarious individuals who mean to do us harm."

"Huh?" said Tater.

"No posters," said Fred, picking up on Mehitabel's

sense of urgency. "We could say that these guys were left without a home after Hurricane Adelaide."

"It's true," said Mehitabel, "we were. Then again, we didn't live in what you would call a home *before* the hurricane, but I see no need to be that specific when passing along information to your human friends."

Tater looked confused. But he reported the information as best he could.

"Abby? These cats lost their homes in the hurricane. I think they blew away. Or were washed out to sea. It's a miracle they're still alive."

Jenny came back into the cottage.

"They both lost their homes," Abby told her. "In the hurricane."

"Another update from Tater?" said Jenny.

"Sort of. His thoughts are kind of jumbled right now."

"Fine. Dr. Appleman will check them out this afternoon. For now, let's wake up Clarence, Barney, and Mister Cookiepants. Leo sent me an action sequence from the script. Seems the space aliens are back."

"The squirrels?" said Abby. She sounded excited. "From *Dog Squad*, season three, episode seven?"

"Yep."

Fred wagged his tail. He'd had fun working with Nutty and Squiggy on that show.

Jenny bent down to talk to Squeak, Yakster, and Mehitabel.

"This time the aliens have kidnapped a kitten. That's you, Squeak. If the Cat Crew is going to rescue her, those cats need to learn some slick new moves—and fast!"

CAT CREW

EPISODE 1

"A FURMIDABLE NEW FELINE FORCE"

ACTION SEQUENCE

REHEARSAL ROUGH CUT

ANIMAL TRAINER'S NOTE: This is where we are after two full weeks of intensive training. —Jenny Yen

No animals were harmed in the making of this film.® —Lily Morel, American Humane Film & TV Unit

TATER, THE PUPPY, points to an elevated platform on the far bank of the turbulent whitewater rapids.

"Look, Duke!" he barks. "It's those same

evil alien squirrels who tried to kidnap me! They've got Princess Squeak!"

Duke thrusts out his chest heroically. The sunlight rims his head, also heroically.

"So," says Duke, "those intergalactic rodents came back for another taste of my fur-ry, eh?"

The leader of the space squirrels, decked out in his miniature space suit, shakes his tiny fist in Duke's general direction.

"We are taking this royal kitten back to our planet, where she will teach us all she knows about her mortal enemy—dogs!"

"We don't all hate you, Duke," says Mehitabel, the leader of the Cat Crew.

"But we sure hate thinking about what they might do to Princess Squeak!" adds Yakster, her frisky (and chatty) sidekick. "Plus, she's wearing that diamond-encrusted collar. It's been in her royal family for centuries."

"Fear not, friends," says Mehitabel. "When calamity calls . . ."

"Call in Cat Crew!" reply her four teammates—some more enthusiastically than others. In fact, one cat is yawning.

"I need a nap," he says.

"We'll do this without Clarence," says Mehitabel.

"But how?" says Duke, sizing up the situation. "They have young Princess Squeak high up on that elevated platform. The only way to rescue her is by crossing these raging rapids."

"There's a rail spanning the river like a balance beam!" says Yakster.

"And I have incredible balance!" cries Mehitabel.

Duke watches with amazement as Mehitabel puts one paw in front of the other and effortlessly scampers along the narrow beam. Yakster scurries across after her. The music becomes even more dramatic, with lots of DUN-DUN-DUH, DUN-DUN-DUHs.

The other three members of the Cat Crew do not follow.

Clarence is napping. Barney is chasing butterflies. Mister Cookiepants is rummaging in the bushes, looking for a snack.

Meanwhile, up on the elevated landing pad, Princess Squeak is trembling with fear.

"Help me!" she peeps. "Cat Crew? Save me!"

"Hang on, Your Highness!" cries Mehitabel. Having crossed the gurgling stream, she now has to scoot through a narrow pipe.

She emerges directly beneath the twenty-foot pole holding up the squirrels' lofty perch. Mehitabel wraps her front legs around the slender shaft and scoot-shinnies up it with ease.

"Hang in there, Princess!" she shouts.

When Mehitabel is halfway up the pole, Yakster crawls out of the pipe near its base.

"Hey, look," he says. "There's freeze-dried salmon treats at this end!"

"Um, you're not supposed to say that part out loud," Duke hollers across the roaring river.

"The treats are a secret," adds Tater.

"There're secret treats?" says Mister Cookiepants.

Suddenly, he is interested. Furry belly swaying, he clumsily lopes across the balance beam and tries to scoot into the pipe. But his bottom is too wide. His head and shoulders go in, but his fuzzy butt sticks out.

He lets loose a muffled cry. "Help!"

"Uh-oh," says Barney. "Ol' Cookiepants is in trouble."

"Trouble?" says Duke. "When trouble calls, it's Dog Squad to the rescue!"

Duke races across the slick balance beam to rescue Mister Cookiepants.

It's so wet, he slips and tumbles into the stream just as Mehitabel hisses at the space squirrels, who leap into a nearby tree while Mehitabel and Squeak spring off the elevated platform and parachute to the ground, where Yakster rolls around in a bed of leafy plants resembling sprigs of peppermint.

"It's catnip, you guys!" he says, sounding goofy. "Catnip!"

Tater lifts his leg and waters a shrub.

Duke climbs out of the river and shakes himself dry, splattering Barney and Clarence.

They hiss, flick out their claws, and swipe at the air.

Off in the distance, somebody screams "Cut!"

The scene ends.

"WELL," SCRUFFY SAID to Fred, "that's definitely rated D for disaster."

Scruffy had come up from Brooklyn with Mr. Espinosa to look at the rough cut Jenny had pieced together after two weeks of rehearsing for the new show's first episode. Fred, Scruffy, Tater, and all the cats were sprawled on the carpeted floor of Jenny's living room watching the video on Jenny's flat-screen TV.

Fred remembered a glorious night in this same room when everyone celebrated his first triumphant appearance as Duke on *Dog Squad*. Watching the rehearsal footage of the riverside rescue scene, he felt like he'd gone from a hero to a zero. This new show wasn't working. And if it didn't work, all the animals on the ranch might soon be out of a job. Everybody said *Seal Team Seven* was going to crush *Dog Squad*. If that happened and *Cat Crew* was a stinker, Jenny might have to find new homes for her dogs and cats and other animals—just like she had to do when Fred's Broadway show shut down. His newfound family might be scattered to the wind. They might never see each other again.

"I think six cats is too many, Leo," said Jenny when the lights came up in the room. "It's almost impossible to choreograph that kind of chaos."

"But it has to be a cat *crew*," said Mr. Espinosa. "It needs to be bigger than the Dog *Squad*."

"Actually," sniffed Mister Cookiepants, "cat *clowder* would be the more correct terminology."

"We could add more special effects to fill in the gaps in the action," said Mr. Espinosa, sighing wearily and rubbing his eyes. "Of course, that means more money. And we're already over budget."

"On the bright side, the new stray cats are terrific," said Abby, who, in Fred's experience, always tried to find the silver lining in any cloudy situation. "Did you see how Mehitabel climbed that pole?"

Fred had. It was definitely something he could never do. And not just the climbing bit. The being-up-high part looked even more terrifying!

"And," Abby went on, "Yakster matched Mehitabel, move for move."

"Until he got distracted by the salmon treats and the catnip," said Mr. Espinosa with another sigh.

"Sorry," said Yakster. "My bad."

"You'll do better next time," said Mehitabel. "Remember, Einstein is counting on us. We must rescue him and reunite our family."

"Family?" said Yakster. "He's an Abyssinian. I'm a Siamese."

"And yet," said Mehitabel, "together we are a family. One we chose for ourselves."

Mehitabel turned to Clarence, Barney, and Mister Cookiepants.

"And you three? Remember: Teamwork will make the dream work. We must all give our all."

"You tell 'em," peeped Squeak.

"Oh, I will. In much the same firm but fair way Catherine the Great told me and her two hundred and ninety-nine other cats that we needed to up our game protecting the priceless art treasures in the Winter Palace. For there were many rats and mice determined to nibble upon their canvas and gilded frames. This, of course, was in the late 1750s. . . ."

Scruffy looked to Fred. "How old is this cat?"

Fred shrugged. He had no idea.

"You three have a very sweet thing going here," Mehitabel continued. "Cozy beds. A roof over your head on rainy nights. A never-ending kibble bowl buffet. But this could all be gone in a flash. Don't believe me? Ask He of the Velvety Paws."

"Who's that?" asked Clarence, sounding a little less bored.

"Catherine the Great's American cat. He dared scratch the face of a lady-in-waiting and was soon banished from the palace, perhaps to Siberia, where he, no doubt, wished he had warm mittens instead of velvety paws."

Barney gulped. "Are you saying Jenny is gonna toss us out if'n we don't start jumpin' through hoops for her?"

"It's possible. We need to pull together and work as a team! A true Cat Crew."

"Nice pep talk, furball," said Cha-Cha the chow chow as she pranced into the TV room. "I wondered where you all were."

"We were watching a ruff cut of *Cat Crew*," said Tater. "Get it? A *ruff* cut?"

"Got it," said Cha-Cha. "Didn't really want it, but I got it. Was it as bad as rumor has it?"

"It's a work in progress," said Fred.

"It stinks," said Squeak, because she was a kitten and hadn't yet learned how to sugarcoat the truth. "Smells worse than a clump of week-old poop."

Cha-Cha elevated her snout. "What a shame. Because, news flash, they say *Seal Team Seven* flippered its way into a dead heat with the *Dog Squad* season finale. That . . . *thing* . . . you shot in Paris."

Fred gulped a little. Was he going to be banished to Siberia like that cat in Mehitabel's story?

"Don't worry," said Tater. "*Cat Crew* will be a smash hit!"

"Doubtful," sniffed Cha-Cha. "If I were you, I'd start worrying about looking good for your next adoption. Me? I'll be fine. Why? Because I'm unbelievably gorgeous. Ciao."

She strutted out of the room, her fluffy hair swinging and swaying.

"Who, pray tell, is that furry windbag?" asked Mehitabel.

"Nobody," said Scruffy.

"She's Cha-Cha," said Fred. "And she might be right. If this show flops . . ."

Mehitabel placed a comforting paw on Fred's front paw.

"Don't worry, Fred. This show shall be a smash, boffo hit!"

She turned once more to the cats.

"Ladies and gentlemen, we have much work to do! But do it we shall. For we are the Cat Crew. We just need a major cattitude adjustment!"

MEANWHILE, INSIDE THE MANSION down the lane, Kitty Bitteridge was pedaling her high-tech exercise bike and fuming at an *Entertainment Nightly* story displayed on its video screen.

"*Cat Crew*?" she hissed as the electronic bike did most of the pedaling for her. "A spin-off from *Dog Squad*? The nerve! Now Jenny Yen thinks *she* can train cats?"

"Pah!" said Dimitri, who was hoisting a heavy leather medicine ball and dropping it to the floor. "Does she wield the power of the collar? Nyet. Does she have the cat-controlling manipulation of the leopard gloves at her fingertips? Double nyet."

"How dare she!" Kitty's stationary bike's wheels spun even faster. "This is my time to shine!"

"Pah!" Dimitri said again, thudding his medicine ball down on the gym mat for emphasis. "She is a foolish dog trainer. What does she know of cats? Nichego! Nothing!"

"Where is it?" muttered Miss Bitteridge. She swiped her finger across the computerized bicycle's monitor. Sweat was dribbling down her nose and plinking on the glass. "Where is it?!?"

"What are you looking for, Miss Kitty?"

"This! The one truly important story. The one about *America's Most Amazingly Talented Animals*!"

"Ah! What does this one truly important story say?"

"That we are to be one of the acts featured in the competition!"

"Da. But we have known this for many days, Miss Kitty."

"So? I like seeing my name in print. Especially when they spell it correctly. It's time we spring into action, Dimitri! The prize will be one million dollars. Of course, I don't care about the money . . ."

"I do."

"Don't be a fool, Dimitri. Fame is the more valuable prize. With fame comes glory. And with glory come respect, honor, and accolades. We *will* win that Pawscar Award next year."

"I still think one million dollars is nothing to be sneezing at."

"Fine, Dimitri. When we win, you can keep the one million dollars. You will be filthy rich. Not as filthy rich as me, but filthy enough."

"Excellent. I look forward to this filthy richness. But

now we have work to do. We must perfect the drill team routine. The one where the cats form the pyramid like so many American cheerleaders!"

"Yes, Dimitri," said Miss Bitteridge distractedly. She switched off her electronic bicycle.

Dimitri made a sour face as he lowered his hefty medicine ball to the floor. "Pardon me, Miss Kitty, but you said that 'Yes' rather distractedly."

"Because I *am* distracted! No. Worse. I'm worried. About our neighbors' schemes."

"They have schemes?"

"What if, as a publicity stunt for their new *Cat Crew* show, the goody-goody do-gooders next door decide to enter *their* cats in the *America's Most Amazingly Talented Animals* competition? After all, *AMATA* is on the same network as *Dog Squad*! What if, in the finals, we must face the cats from *Cat Crew*?"

Dimitri gasped. "Tree sticks! Two cat acts in the same contest? This would not be good, Miss Kitty. Do you ever see two dance crews make it to the finals of *America's Got Talent*? No. You do not. Two acts shooting flaming arrows while riding unicycles? Nyet. Only one. A copycat cat team could destroy us. And hunger is no auntie; it will not give you a pie."

Miss Bitteridge looked at Dimitri with elevated eyebrows. "Is that another one of those Russian expressions I'll never understand?"

"Da," said Dimitri. "Russian is a very colorful language. Our words are like a box of crayons. The big one with one hundred and fifty-two colors and the convenient crayon sharpener. But whatever words you choose, this *Cat Crew* could steal all the thunder and glory and prize money that should belong to us!"

Miss Bitteridge dabbed the sweat off her face with a tiger-striped towel.

"This must not happen, Dimitri. Fluff up your tuxedo shirt. I'll put on my best kitty-print dress. It's time we paid our neighbors a visit. We have some spying to do!"

25

FRED AND THE OTHERS were still in the living room when the doorbell rang.

Scruffy put his paws up on a windowsill and peeked through the curtains.

"It's a strange red-haired lady. She's carrying a jiggly fish on a platter. There's a mustachioed man with her. I think he might be a disco dancer."

"Jiggly fish?" said Mister Cookiepants. He heaved himself up to the window with a grunt. "Mmmm. Poached salmon with a delightful sour-cream-and-dill sauce."

Squeak, the kitten, hid behind a chair. "Does the lady with red hair have bright red lips?"

Fred went to the window on the other side of the front door.

"Yes," he reported.

"Yikes!" screeched Squeak. "Don't open that door."

"I concur," said Mehitabel. "Those two are nothing but trouble. We must hide."

The doorbell rang again.

"Coming!" called Jenny from off in the kitchen, where she and Mr. Espinosa were drinking coffee.

"This way," said Fred, heading to the closet. "My friend Reginald taught me how to gum a doorknob to twist it open."

Fred made the same moves Reginald, the golden retriever, had made in a famous real estate commercial. He pulled the door open.

Squeak streaked across the room and skidded into the closet. Mehitabel and Yakster dashed in after her. Fred and Scruffy nudged the closet shut just as Jenny opened the front door.

"Hello!" cooed the redheaded woman on the porch. "I don't believe we've met. I'm your next-door neighbor. Kitty Bitteridge. This is my chauffeur, Dimitri Kuznetsov."

"Hello," said the man with the mustache, dipping his head and clicking his heels together. "We have brought for you the fish."

The woman who called herself Kitty stepped through the door before Jenny invited her in.

"It's for the cats," she said. "We understand you're doing a new show. *Cat Crew,* I believe it's called?"

"Yes. Uh, here. Let me take that platter. I should put the fish in the fridge." Jenny carried the platter out of the living room.

"Dang if that salmon don't smell sweeter than green grass after a thunder boomer," said Barney, wiggling his nose.

While Jenny was out of the room, the two neighbors eyeballed the three cats.

"These cats are to be our competition?" said the mustachioed man. "We have nothing to fear."

"Except that shabby tabby stepping on our toes," said the lady, indicating Mister Cookiepants.

They both giggled.

"Hey," said Barney, "they's a-laughin' at us."

"Who cares?" said Mister Cookiepants. "They brought salmon."

"That dog there?" sneered Miss Bitteridge. "That's the one they call Fred. He plays the brave and heroic Duke. Does he look remotely brave or heroic?"

"Pah! He looks like a queasy coward."

Scruffy yapped and snarled. "Don't listen to them, Fred."

"Yeah," said Tater. "Don't listen."

"Um, it's kind of hard not to," said Fred. "They're standing right there."

Jenny came back into the living room and heard the three dogs grumbling and growling.

"Is everything okay?" she asked.

"Yes," said Miss Bitteridge. "Just admiring your animals. Will these three cats be in *Cat Crew*?"

"Yes. If they want to be. It's really up to them."

The man snorted back a laugh. "Up to them," he muttered.

"And will you also be entering them in the upcoming talent competition?" asked Miss Bitteridge.

"Excuse me?"

"Will your cats be competing on *America's Most Amazingly Talented Animals*?"

"Oh, no," said Jenny. "We can't do that. The network that produces *Dog Squad* and *Cat Crew* is also producing *AMATA*. So it would be a conflict of interest."

"Well, we just wanted to drop by and say hello," said Miss Bitteridge. "It's been too long since we've all been together like this."

"This is the first time we've ever met. Remember?"

"Well, I've been busy. Very, very busy. But we'll definitely have to do this again. Soon. Come along, Dimitri. We have work to do!"

26

"OKAY, GUYS," SAID Abby, coming into the living room after the uninvited guests had left. "It's time to go back to work. Scruffy? Mr. Espinosa wants to take you for a walk. He's in the kitchen with Aunt Jenny."

"Leo must be having writer's block again," said Scruffy.

He trotted off to the kitchen.

Abby turned to Fred, Tater, and the three cats from the cottage. "Aunt Jenny has some new moves she'd like you guys to learn right away."

Abby unzipped a pair of cat carriers and looked around the room.

"Where are Squeak, Mehitabel, and Yakster?"

"In the closet!" barked Tater. "They're hiding!"

Abby touched her temple.

"In the closet?" said Abby. "How'd that happen?"

Fred scampered back to the closet and did his door-opening trick again.

Mehitabel stuck out her head.

"Is the coast clear?" she asked.

"Yep," said Fred. "The neighbor lady left. Her chauffeur, too."

Mehitabel pranced out of the closet, her tail held high. "Yakster? Squeak? Olly olly oxen free."

Yakster and Squeak crept out of the closet a little more cautiously.

"Phew," peeped Squeak. She turned to face Clarence, Barney, and Mister Cookiepants. "Whatever you do, stay away from that lady. You do NOT want to be one of her cats."

"Speak for yourself," said Mister Cookiepants. "I could get used to poached salmon on a regular basis."

"Then you'd have to get used to—the collar!"

"Oh, I don't mind wearin' a collar," said Barney. "Especially if'n it has one of them jingly bells."

"You guys?" said Abby as she attempted to corral the six cats and coax them into the open carriers. "We need to go out to the barn. Aunt Jenny and the Babkows have set up a really cool obstacle course so you can work out all the moves for the rest of the rescue scene."

Every time she approached Clarence, Barney, or Mister Cookiepants, they skittered away.

"You need to practice your moves!" Abby lunged at

Mister Cookiepants. He darted out of her grasp. "Once you save Squeak, you have to escape from the alien squirrels who come chasing after you on hover bikes."

"No thank you," said Mister Cookiepants. "Escaping usually requires running."

He scooted under a couch.

"The only escape I'm interested in," said Clarence, "is into my bed."

He trotted toward the back door.

Abby tried to grab him.

He slipped out of her grip, spun around, and hissed.

"Clarence? This is important."

He hissed again. Abby backed off. She turned to Barney.

"I'm with Clarence." He swatted at Abby. "It's nap time. You try to stop me, I'm gonna jerk a knot in your tail faster than green grass through a goose!"

Fred turned to Mehitabel.

"What does that even mean?"

She shook her head. "I have no idea."

Barney and Clarence hightailed it out of the house through the flapping doggy door. Mister Cookiepants burrowed deeper under the sofa.

Abby looked down at Mehitabel, Yakster, and Squeak.

She exhaled sadly. "So, do you three want to hide under the furniture or swat at me?"

"No," said Mehitabel proudly. "We're very interested

in learning all that you and your aunt Jenny have to teach us." She turned to Yakster. "Come along. You and I must learn how to *rescue* Squeak from the squirrels!"

"And then we'll rescue Einstein, right?" whispered Yakster. "This is rescue rehearsal for that other rescue, right?"

"Indeed," said Mehitabel with a wink. "This is practice for our upcoming family reunion!"

27

CAT CREW

EPISODE 1

"A FURMIDABLE NEW FELINE FORCE"

ACTION SEQUENCE

REHEARSAL ROUGH CUT #2

ANIMAL TRAINER'S NOTE: This is where we are after <u>three</u> full weeks of intensive training. —Jenny Yen

No animals were harmed in the making of this film.® —Lily Morel, American Humane Film & TV Unit

TATER, THE PUPPY, points to an elevated platform at the tip of a twenty-foot pole on the far bank of the turbulent whitewater rapids.

"Look, Duke!" he barks. "It's those same evil alien squirrels who tried to kidnap me! They've got Princess Squeak!"

Duke thrusts out his chest heroically. The sunlight rims his head, also heroically.

"So," says Duke, with a great deal of gusto, "those intergalactic rodents came back for another taste of my fur-ry, eh?"

The leader of the space squirrels shakes his tiny fist in Duke's direction.

"You fools! We are taking this royal kitten back to our planet, where she will teach us all she knows about her mortal enemy—dogs!"

"We don't all hate you, Duke," says Mehitabel, the leader of the two-member Cat Crew.

"But we sure hate thinking about what they might do to Princess Squeak!" adds Yakster, her frisky (and chatty) sidekick. "Plus, she's wearing that diamond-encrusted collar. It's been in the royal family for centuries."

"Fear not, Yakster," says Mehitabel. "When calamity calls . . ."

"Call in Cat Crew!" replies Yakster.

"But how?" says Duke, sizing up the situation. "They have Princess Squeak on that elevated platform."

"Elevated platforms are what we do best!" says Mehitabel, squinting courageously at the horizon. "Come on, Yakster!"

Duke watches with amazement as Mehitabel and Yakster valiantly scamper across an extremely narrow beam bridging the raging rapids. The music becomes even more dramatic, with lots of DUN-DUN-DUH, DUN-DUN-DUHs.

Meanwhile, up on the elevated spaceship landing pad, Princess Squeak trembles with fear.

"Help me!" Squeak peeps. "Cat Crew? Save me!"

"Hang on, Your Highness," cries Mehitabel. She has crossed the gurgling stream and must scoot through a narrow pipe.

Mehitabel emerges from the far end of the iron tunnel and is directly beneath the twenty-foot pole holding up the squirrels' perch. She wraps her front legs around the slender shaft and scoot-shinnies up it with ease.

"Hang in there, Princess!" she shouts.

Now Yakster boldly emerges from the pipe

and darts to the riverbank. "Come on over, Duke! The water's shallow!"

Tater hops onto Duke's back. Duke leaps into the stream and doggy-paddles across.

Up on the platform, Mehitabel swats at the alien squirrels with claws fully extended.

"Princess Squeak? You're coming with me."

Mehitabel grabs Squeak by the scruff of the neck. She leaps off the platform with the kitten safely clasped in her mouth.

They plummet fast . . .

. . . and land on Duke's back—just as Tater leaps off Duke and lands on Yakster.

"Let's hightail it out of here, Cat Crew!" says Duke.

They take off running. They zig and zag around rocks and tree trunks. They leap over fallen logs. The alien squirrels chase them on flying speeder bikes!

"Time to use a tree for something besides a pee!" shouts Duke.

He skirts closer to a tree, brushing its bark.

Suddenly, there is a loud boom overhead.

The flying squirrels bash into the tree and crash.

"Good thing they were wearing their helmets!" says Mehitabel. "Something you should always do when riding your bike!"

A voice cries, "Cut! We got it!"

The scene ends.

28

"NICE ACTION SEQUENCE," said Scruffy.

"Thanks," said Fred. "I think it works."

Scruffy had come up to the Second Chance Ranch with Mr. Espinosa again to see the latest edit of the new show's stunts.

Jenny had just screened a tighter version of the rescue and escape sequence. Lily Morel, the representative of the American Humane Film & TV Unit, had already certified that "no animals were harmed in the making of this film." Ms. Morel was always on the set when Jenny worked with her animals.

"If I may quote your sheepherding friend Nala," said Mehitabel with a great deal of pride, "I daresay we were pawsome."

"It's a real claw-biter!" jabbered Yakster. "We should call ourselves the Fast and the Fur-rious!"

"I just hope Mr. Espinosa is happy," said Fred, eyeing the producer.

If *Cat Crew* was a hit, everything could stay the same at the ranch. All the dogs and cats could keep on working. Fred wouldn't have to say a sad goodbye to any members of his new family.

But Mr. Espinosa was quiet.

Too quiet.

"So?" Jenny finally asked.

"It's great," said Mr. Espinosa.

Fred breathed a sigh of relief.

"But . . ."

Okay. Fred probably did that relieved breathing a little too soon.

"Oh boy," said Scruffy. "Here it comes . . ."

"I hate buts," said Fred, which made Scruffy giggle.

"You said *butts*."

Yakster giggled a little too. Fred didn't. He was laser-focused on Jenny and Mr. Espinosa.

"What's wrong, Leo?" asked Jenny.

He tossed up both hands. "Sorry. It's just not a cat *crew*. It's not even a cat squad. It's a cat team. A dynamic cat duo. It's Catman and Robin. I wanted the Avengers. Where's Clarence, the cat we used in that *Dog Squad* episode?"

"He doesn't have the right stuff," Jenny said with a sigh. "Neither does Barney or Mister Cookiepants. They're just not interested."

"Can you find new cats at the shelter?"

"Maybe. But that would only slow us down even more."

Mr. Espinosa rubbed his face. "Okay. I'll try to buy us some more time. The network really wanted this show fast, Jenny. *Seal Team Seven* is hitting us hard. Rumor has it they're working on a spin-off of their own. Probably something with dolphins."

"Cats don't do fast, Leo," said Jenny. "Sorry."

"It's true," said Yakster. "We're more stealthy than speedy. Unless we're chasing stuff like—"

Suddenly, Mr. Espinosa's phone rang.

"Uh-oh," he said, studying the phone's screen. "It's Bob. At the network."

"Buy us that extra training time," said Jenny.

"I'll try." He took the call. "Hey, Bob. Oh yeah. Things look fantastic. Sure. What's the favor? Well, that's going to eat into the rehearsal schedule. Tell you what— Jenny and Fred will do it, but we're gonna need to bump back the *Cat Crew* premiere. Just a little. Jenny will even bring a cat. Perfect. Talk to you soon."

Mr. Espinosa ended the call.

"What was all that?" asked Jenny.

"I bought us some time," said Mr. Espinosa.

"And?"

"The network needs you and Duke to be celebrity guest judges for *America's Most Amazingly Talented Animals*. The live finals show is tomorrow night down in New York. Take one of the cats, too."

"Mehitabel," said Jenny. "She's the smartest."

Mehitabel turned to Yakster. "That's just one woman's opinion."

Yakster shrugged. "It's okay. Age before beauty, as they say. And you're on, what, your ninety-ninth life?"

"Unfortunately, I have lost count."

"It'll be a great promotion for *Cat Crew*," Mr. Espinosa told Jenny. "Once, you know, we put together a crew of cats."

"We're working on it, Leo."

"Well, work faster, Jenny. Please?"

LATE THAT AFTERNOON, when there was no more work to be done on *Cat Crew*, Mehitabel and Yakster slipped out of the cat cottage.

They traipsed across the horse pasture, crossed the creek, and quietly crept onto the lush lawn surrounding the mammoth mansion.

"We must make contact with Einstein," said Mehitabel. "Let him know that we have neither abandoned nor forsaken him. Assure him that we are but in training, honing our rescue and escape skills."

"And starring in a TV show," added Yakster.

"That's just part of our master plan. The more we work with Jenny, the more strategy and tactics we shall possess when the time comes to free our friend."

"It's been weeks since we last saw Einstein," said Yakster as they tiptoed through the soft grass. "That's almost a month. I think. I never did understand that whole calendar dealio. It's either sunup or sundown. Summer, fall, winter, or—"

"Yakster?"

"Yeah, Mehitabel?"

"We should shift into our silent and stealthy approach mode. Remember how we do that?"

"Yeah. I remember. No, wait. I forgot. I—"

"Shhhh!"

"Right. Gotcha. Not another word out of me. I'm making like a phone and going into silent mode."

Finally, with Yakster all blathered out, they approached the windows looking down into the red-haired lady's gymnasium.

But the basement workout room was empty. No one was on the balance beams, parallel bars, or tumbling mats. The lights had all been turned off.

"They're gone!" said a voice above the cats. "Every last meowing one of 'em. I say good riddance to bad birdseed."

It was a bright blue bird, high up in a tree.

"Don't get any ideas about climbing up here to nibble on my beak," said the bird. "I'll fly away and you'll just be two cats up a tree!"

"Actually," said Mehitabel, "we're very honorable cats. We would never think of 'nibbling' on you."

"Ha! Tell it to my cousin Louie. He lost his tail feathers to one of those zombie cats. The lady with the twiddling fingers sent one of her I-be-seein'-ya monsters chasing after him."

"I believe you meant to say 'Abyssinian,' " said Mehitabel with a friendly smile.

"That's what I did say. I-be-seein'-ya, which is what Louie said to that cat, right after it bit him in his hiney."

"Do you, perchance, have any idea where the cats and their keepers have gone?"

"Yeah," said the bird. "Away. And hopefully, they won't be comin' back anytime soon."

"But our friend is with them," whimpered Yakster.

"We used to prowl an alley together," added Mehitabel.

"Whereabouts?" asked the bird.

"New York City," said Mehitabel, wistfully remembering happier days.

"Oh, now that you mention it, that's where the lady with the twitchy fingers told the curly-haired guy to drive her and the kitty cats."

"Aha! Thank you, my fine feathered friend."

"I ain't your friend! I'm a bird, remember? We hate each other!"

The bird flapped away.

"We're in luck, Yakster!" exclaimed Mehitabel. "As you know, Mr. Espinosa wants Fred and me to go down to New York City to judge that animal talent show. We can nose around town and sniff out Einstein!"

"Yeah," said Yakster excitedly. "It should be easy. Einstein has a very cheesy butt. He's the cheesiest!"

THE NEXT AFTERNOON, Fred and Mehitabel rode with Abby and Jenny down to New York City.

"*America's Most Amazingly Talented Animals* is doing its big finale at Radio City Music Hall!" Abby told them. "I'm so excited."

"This'll be fun," added Jenny from behind the steering wheel.

Fred was looking forward to the big night in New York City too.

He wasn't nervous about the live broadcast. All he, Jenny, and Mehitabel had to do was sit behind a table as part of the judges' panel. If there were any comments to be made, Jenny would be the one making them. Sure, Fred might occasionally bark and Mehitabel might meow once or twice, but this was, basically, Jenny's show.

"Fred?" said Mehitabel when they reached the congested streets of Manhattan. "I wonder if I might ask a favor?"

"Sure. What's up?"

"There is something in New York City that I would like to retrieve. After we complete our duties for Jenny, I was hoping you might employ your incredible powers of smell to sniff about for my lost . . . item."

"I don't know. Jenny doesn't really like us roaming off on our own."

"Of course, of course. But perhaps you could follow a certain scent when it's time for your final dog walk prior to our departure?"

"Okay. That might work.

Abby usually lets me pick my own path. What am I sniffing for?"

"Something extremely cheesy."

Fred gasped. "Did you lose a bag of Snausages?"

Mehitabel smiled. "I'll give you more details later."

Jenny piloted the van up to the curb outside the world-famous Radio City Music Hall. It was spectacular! So many buzzing neon lights!

Abby clipped a leash to Fred's collar. Jenny leashed Mehitabel. A stagehand would park the van.

After stopping by "hair and makeup" (where Fred and Mehitabel both got a good brushing), they were escorted into the biggest auditorium Fred had ever seen. The crowd cheered when they saw Duke.

Fred gave his fans a happy wag of his fluffed-out tail.

He, Jenny, and Mehitabel were led to their places in the middle of the long judges' desk.

The Grammy-award-winning singer Rachel Christensen was on the panel. So was Ella Olivia Posner—the YouTube star who'd adopted the original Duke.

"Hello, Jenny!" she said.

"Hiya, Ella! How's Duke?"

"Loving Hollywood. He spends a lot of time in my pool. Is that the new Duke?"

"That's right. This is Fred."

Fred gave her a happy, panting smile.

Posner squiggled her finger in a zigzag. "The lightning bolt of white on his forehead goes the wrong way."

Jenny laughed. "No. I think Duke's the one who got it backward."

That made Fred's smile widen.

"Jenny certainly loves you," whispered Mehitabel.

"Yeah," said Fred. "She certainly does."

And he loved her.

Jenny had given Fred the one thing every dog wants but can never give themselves: a home. That was why Fred couldn't let Jenny down. He had to make sure *Cat Crew* was a hit—even if he had to do more stunts and action and dialogue than all the cats combined!

The TV talent show started.

"Let's meet our judges!" said the master of ceremonies. "With us from the smash hit *Dog Squad,* put your hands together for animal trainer Jenny Yen and the star you all know and love—Duke!"

The audience cheered and applauded.

"Plus, joining Jenny and Duke, one of the bright new stars from the upcoming *Dog Squad* spin-off, *Cat Crew*! Say hello to Mehitabel!"

The auditorium erupted with whistles and cheers.

Mehitabel took a bow.

"Thank you. Thank you," she said. "You are too kind."

The other two judges were introduced, and the amazing animal acts took the stage.

The geese honking Broadway show tunes were hilarious!

The turtle gymnastics team was hard to see and kind of slow.

And then ten cats, looking almost exactly alike, marched onto the stage.

Fred immediately recognized their trainer.

It was Kitty Bitteridge. Their next-door neighbor. Her leopard-spotted gloves were trimmed with what Fred hoped was fake fur.

"Thank goodness we were fluffed and buffed for this event," Mehitabel whispered to Fred. "The redheaded lady doesn't seem to recognize me from our previous encounter behind her home."

"Is that real fur?" wondered Fred. "On her gloves?"

"Most likely," sighed Mehitabel. "Either way, we can call off our search. What was lost has now been found."

"What do you mean?"

"The third Abyssinian from the left. That's whom I was hoping to retrieve. It's my dear friend Einstein."

31

FRED DIDN'T WANT to say anything rude to Mehitabel, but her friend Einstein looked like he'd seen better days.

His eyes were glassy marbles. There was no twitch in his whiskers. No bounce in his step. He and the other nine Abyssinians sat stock-still, staring straight ahead, while their trainer, Miss Kitty Bitteridge, faced the panel of judges.

"Tell us a little about yourself," said Rachel Christensen, the singer.

"We're the Swing Cats from Wilford, Connecticut."

"That's near the shore?"

"Correct." She grinned. "Very close to Jenny Yen's Second Chance Ranch, as a matter of fact."

Jenny smiled politely.

"Do they still have that amusement park with the Ferris wheel?" asked the YouTube star.

"Who wants to know about that?" joked the singer.

"Me!"

The audience laughed.

"Yes," said Miss Bitteridge. "Oceanside Park is still open."

"I shot a video there once."

"So, Miss Kitty," said Ms. Christensen, "what are you going to do for us today?"

"Amaze and astound you! Show our *Dog Squad* friends what *our* cat crew can do."

Fred's ears perked up. It sounded like a challenge.

"Wooo!" the audience cheered. They liked a challenge too.

"Let's see what you've got!" said Ms. Christensen.

"With pleasure."

Prerecorded rockabilly music started playing.

"That's 'Stray Cat Strut,'" Mehitabel whispered to Fred. "It's a classic tune celebrating the life of a legendary alley cat whom, unfortunately, I never had the pleasure of meeting."

Kitty Bitteridge flicked up her gloves and the ten cats went to work.

They marched back and forth on

a balance beam, scooting under or leaping over the cat coming from the opposite direction.

The crowd cheered.

Miss Bitteridge twiddled her fingertips and the cats did ten synchronized sideways somersaults to the floor.

When she raised her hands as if she were conducting an orchestra, the ten cats started dancing. Her finger twitches were followed by all sorts of incredible dips and jitterbug moves.

"That's amazing!" gushed the singer.

"That's impossible," muttered Jenny, gawking in openmouthed disbelief.

The cats flew into a gymnastics routine. Hopping sideways over each other. Rolling and tumbling and leaping through hoops. Miss Bitteridge orchestrated it all with a flurry of finger flutters.

Fred made eye contact with Einstein. He'd never seen such sadness. Not even on a basset hound.

After the ten cats leapt through ten plastic rings,

they tipped them over and used them as Hula-Hoops to swirl around their hips.

As the foot-stomping dance music rose toward its big finish, the audience members were on their feet, clapping along. Kitty Bitteridge swept up both hands to make a grand gesture.

The ten cats scurried together to form a pyramid with four on the bottom level, three on the second, two on the third. The final cat sprang up and landed at the peak. It stood on its hind legs and triumphantly raised both its front paws!

"We call it our purr-a-mid!" proclaimed Kitty Bitteridge.

The crowd went wild!

"I've never seen anything like it!" cheered Rachel Christensen.

"Spectacular!" shouted Ella Olivia Posner. "Hey, Jenny—can your Cat Crew do that?"

Jenny was smiling, but Fred could tell—her smile was shaky.

"Well," she said with a nervous laugh, "*Cat Crew* isn't really a dance show."

But it could be, thought Fred. *It could be!*

FRED HAD TO do something. Fast.

The Swing Cats were making Jenny look bad.

Ella Olivia Posner smirked. Probably because she knew her dog, the real Duke, would never let a chorus line of ten sneaky cats embarrass Jenny and the whole Second Chance Ranch like the Swing Cats just did!

What would Duke do? Steal the spotlight! Take it back for Jenny and his family!

Fred could dance. He did a funny one with a Chihuahua named Chico when he was in the animal shelter before Jenny and Abby rescued him. He'd once done the same sort of dance to save the day at a pet store grand opening, too.

Well, it was time to save the day again.

Fred leapt out of his seat, sailed over the judges' table, and landed at center stage.

"Fred?!" shouted Jenny. "What are you doing?"

Saving the ranch! Fred wanted to bark. *Saving my home the way you saved me!*

But he was too busy busting a move.

The ten Abyssinian cats hissed at him. Kitty Bitteridge narrowed her eyes and glared. But she didn't dare step in to stop Fred because the show was being broadcast live. Millions of people were watching her. Millions were watching Fred, too.

No, they were watching Duke!

And Duke could dance better than any cat!

"Fred?" Mehitabel zipped onto the stage. "What on earth do you think you're doing, my friend?"

"I'm saving the Second Chance Ranch! We can't let these Swing Cats make Jenny look bad!"

"Very well," sighed Mehitabel. "If you insist."

She sprang up and landed on top of Fred's bobbing head, where she shot up both her front paws like the cat at the top of the Abyssinian pyramid.

The crowd laughed hysterically and pointed at Fred and Mehitabel.

Some of the Swing Cats seemed to be snickering too, their shoulders shuddering. Kitty Bitteridge? Delight twinkled in her eyes.

"What are *you* doing?" Fred said to Mehitabel through his tense stage smile.

"Lending a paw to your efforts. For no one can save the world alone, Fred. We must be smart enough to know when we need help. Don't forget: We're in this thing together!"

Oh-kay, thought Fred. *But I think this might've been a mistake. I think we just turned ourselves into a laughingstock on national TV. This crowd isn't laughing with us.*

They're laughing at us.

IT WAS AFTER midnight when Fred and Mehitabel rode home to Connecticut in a very quiet van.

Jenny, behind the wheel, said nothing.

Abby, in the front passenger seat, was silent too. Fred hunkered down in his crate. Mehitabel curled up on the warm and fleecy blanket that lined the bottom of her cat carrier.

Is Jenny upset? Fred wondered. *Is she mad at me? Was it a mistake to start dancing on a live TV show in front of millions of viewers? Is she going to stop loving me now?*

Fred looked over at Mehitabel.

"Fear not," the cat purred, as if she could read his mind. "All will be well. I sense Jenny is angrier at the situation than at you or me."

"I hope so," said Fred. "But even though they won the million-dollar grand prize, I feel sorry for your friend and all those other cats in that Swing Cats drill team."

Mehitabel nodded. "As do I, Fred. As do I. For Einstein is family to me."

"Well, then, he's family to me."

"How so? Might I remind you, Einstein is a cat."

"Doesn't matter. He's your family. And you're trying to help me. And Jenny. And everybody at the ranch. That means you and all your family members are part of our family too."

The van's tires hummed along the highway.

Other than that, the ride remained eerily quiet. Jenny didn't even have the radio turned on. Usually, she liked to listen to music during long van trips. But not tonight.

Tonight, she's too busy being mad at me!

Finally, Abby broke the silence.

"Aunt Jenny?"

"Yeah, hon?"

"Are you mad at Fred?"

"What?"

"I'm asking for a friend."

Jenny looked up in the rearview mirror and made eye contact with Fred.

"I'm not mad at Fred or Mehitabel," she said. "I might've done the same thing if I knew how to dance. No, I'm worried about those poor Abyssinians. They didn't look very happy."

"Because," sighed Mehitabel, "they are miserable."

Of course all Jenny heard was an affirmative meow.

Fred was thinking about that sad look in Einstein's

eyes. Mehitabel was right. They had to do something to help him.

"Miss Kitty Bitteridge and I seem to have very different training philosophies," Jenny continued. "I only want my cats doing what they want to do. I have to make the stunts fun. Our neighbor wants her cats to do whatever *she* wants them to do."

"But how does she do it?" wondered Abby.

Jenny shook her head. "I don't know. But, Abby?"

"Yeah?"

"I'm going to find out. And if she's hurting those cats . . ."

"Oh, she is," said Mehitabel.

". . . someone's going to have to put a stop to it!"

The next morning, Jenny had the small TV on in the kitchen as she and Abby prepped three dozen bowls with different kinds of pet food.

Nobody even mentioned Fred and Mehitabel's dance routine on any of the TV talk shows. Not even the entertainment reporter Caitlin Kelly, and she and Fred had done an interview together. Everybody was too busy raving about Kitty Bitteridge and her sensational Swing Cats feline dance and gymnastics troupe.

"They certainly deserved to take home the top prize last night," said one perky TV lady.

"But I have to wonder," said her peppy cohost, a guy named Biff. "What are those ten cats going to buy with their one-million-dollar prize money?"

"Easy, Biff," joked the lady. "Cans and cans of tuna fish!"

Biff chuckled. The audience applauded. Jenny changed the channel.

Scruffy came into the kitchen.

"Morning, everybody," he said. "Nothing for me," he yapped up to Jenny at the kitchen counter. "I already had a bagel with a schmear down in Brooklyn."

"I don't have anything for you, Scruffy," said Jenny as she continued filling food bowls. "I know you and Leo ate before you guys drove up here."

"Whoa," said Scruffy. "Now she's a pet psychic too?"

"No," said Mehitabel. "I believe she saw your cream cheese mustache."

Scruffy licked his upper lip. "Oh yeah. Delicious."

"So, Scruffy," said Yakster, "did you and Mr. Espinosa watch the talent show last night? Fred and Mehitabel did a dance. But all anybody wants to talk about are those other cats. The ten Abyssinian zombies!"

"Yeah. I seen it. Then me and Mr. Espinosa went for a walk. He's really worried about *Seal Team Seven*. Something about their 'numbers' being better than *Dog Squad*'s."

"Hey, Aunt Jenny," said Abby, "check it out. It's a new *Seal Team Seven* promo."

Abby turned up the volume on the TV set.

Kevin, the star of the show, was spinning a ball on his snout.

"Hey, *Seal Team Seven* fans, I've got some exciting news you're going to flipper out over."

Kevin sounded even more macho than Duke.

"We have a brand-new, seal-liously awesome spin-off show coming your way—soon!"

When he said "spin-off," the beach ball spun off his snout.

"It definitely has my seal of approval. Oh, and one more thing—you'll never catch me doing a dance with a cat on top of my head. I'm an action star, not a clown!"

Fred looked at Mehitabel.

"Do you think he was making fun of us?"

"No, Fred," said Mehitabel. "Just you."

MEHITABEL AND YAKSTER trekked with Fred and Scruffy uphill to the cat cottage.

"We need to whip those other three cats into shape," said Mehitabel. "Our spin-off show has to be better than the Seal Team's."

"I've been trying to do that for weeks," said Fred.

"Well, Freddy boy," said Scruffy, "maybe you need a little help."

"But I'm supposed to be Duke. The leader. I lead, they follow."

"Unfortunately," said Mehitabel, "cats don't play follow-the-leader as well as you dogs. We are extremely territorial, each of us claiming a space of our own."

"So," said Yakster, "you need to bring us together slowly. You give us time, we'll eventually work things out. Eventually. Maybe. Can't be one hundred percent certain."

"But you heard the TV," said Fred. "Kevin and *Seal Team Seven* are going to launch their own spin-off series!"

"We need to beat them to the punch!" said Scruffy.

"If we goof up," said Fred, "if we don't deliver a smash hit, we could lose our home. Our family could get broken up."

Mehitabel nodded. "We understand, Fred. This situation reminds me of the dilemma President Lincoln faced on the eve of the Battle of Gettysburg when—"

"Pssst," Yakster whispered to Mehitabel. "Might I have a word with you? In private?"

"Sure, sure," said Scruffy. "Fred and me can take a hint. You two go have your private little kitty-chitty-chat. We'll round up Tater."

"Meet us in front of the cat cottage in five!" said Fred.

The two dogs loped off.

"What is it, Yakster?" said Mehitabel when the two cats were alone.

"Forget Lincoln for a second. What about Einstein? Are we still going to save him? Because that's what we're supposed to be doing up here. We're only hanging out on this fancy-pants ranch so we can learn a few tricks to help us rescue our pal."

Mehitabel sighed. "I concur, Yakster. But you should've seen those ten Abyssinian cats last night. They were like an army of well-trained warriors. We may need a sizable force of our own to free our brother Einstein from their clutches."

"So, what? We try to whip these show-biz cats into shape? Make an army of our own?"

"Precisely. We have much work to do!"

Mehitabel and Yakster trotted up the hill to the cat cottage.

There was a new dog waiting outside its door. A very athletic-looking black-and-white border collie. A shepherd dog they hadn't met before. At least not in real life.

"Wow!" said Yakster. "You're you. You're Nala."

"That's right," said Nala. "I am."

"Are you here to offer us your wise advice and counsel?" asked Mehitabel.

Nala nodded. "Rumor has it *Cat Crew* is in trouble."

"Yeah," said Yakster. "Kind of. I mean, sort of. I mean, yeah. It's in deep doo-doo."

"Well," said Nala, "when trouble calls . . ."

Fred, Scruffy, and Tater arrived just in time to finish that thought.

"It's Dog Squad to the rescue!"

"With the help of the Cat Crew, too!" Mehitabel added.

"Shall we get to work, ladies and gentlemen?" said Nala. "Because champions train while others complain!"

"GOL-DURN!" SHOUTED BARNEY. "This is dadgum fun!"

Jenny was letting the barn cat chase the red dot of a laser pointer up and down a scaffold of platforms she and Mr. Babkow had erected inside the ranch's barn.

"We told you it would be," said Mehitabel.

"See the dot," coached Nala from the sidelines. "Be the dot."

"Are you enjoying your romp, Barney?" asked Mehitabel.

"Shoo-yeah. You got me grinnin' like a possum eatin' a sweet tater."

Fred turned to Yakster.

"He's happy," Yakster translated.

"Riiight," said Fred.

"What'd you say to Barney to wake him up like this?" Scruffy asked Mehitabel.

"Oh, just a little something one of my first owners, a Roman poet named Virgil, told *me* many, many moons ago. 'They can conquer who believe they can.'"

Now Clarence stood up, stretched out his whole body, and pranced over to where Jenny held the laser pointer.

"Yoo-hoo. Laser lady? I believe it's my turn."

His request came out as a series of high-pitched meows.

"I think Clarence wants to do some climbing too!" said Abby.

"How observant," said Clarence sarcastically. "No wonder everyone says the kid's a pet psychic."

Jenny swung the red dot up the scaffolding.

Clarence's eyes locked in on their target. He raced after the glowing speck of light.

"Wow," Fred said to Mehitabel as they watched both Barney and Clarence race up and down the platforms. "I've never seen Clarence be so not-bored before."

"He was given the proper motivation," said Mehitabel.

"And the proper reward!" said Yakster. "That's a freeze-dried salmon cube Jenny's chucking his way!"

Yakster darted up the stairs, chasing after the laser pointer's beam, which Jenny kept flicking back and forth to keep the chase and the hunt interesting.

"This is how we'll do the scene up on the rooftop!" Jenny said to Abby.

"It'll be clawsome!" joked Abby.

Jenny laughed.

Fred smiled. Jenny and Abby both seemed a whole lot happier than they had been at Radio City Music Hall after Fred did his little dance on TV.

"Hang on!" peeped a tiny voice. It was Squeak. "No more naps for me! If you snooze you lose."

"If you three will excuse me," Mehitabel said, with a bow to the stars of *Dog Squad*. "I should also join in the merriment with our new Cat Crew!"

Mehitabel, Yakster, Squeak, Clarence, and Barney chased each other up and down the switchback staircases that connected the platforms rising up to the barn's ceiling. They did what Jenny and her laser pointer urged them to do.

All the cats were having a blast. For the first time, they looked like a team. A true Cat Crew!

All the cats except one.

Mister Cookiepants.

He was miserable.

Look at them. All the running and the chasing and the panting. It makes me want to hock up a hair ball.

As he sat in a dark corner of the barn sulking, inspiration struck.

Those cats who won the big talent show live right next door. And their trainer, the lady with the red hair. She brought us chilled salmon! He licked his chops at the memory. *Maybe she needs a new, unforgettable face. Maybe she needs ME!*

Mister Cookiepants stood up and quietly, very quietly, slipped through the slight opening between the sliding barn doors.

Everyone else was too busy foolishly chasing each other up and down staircases to even notice.

Mister Cookiepants was running away from home.

Because the grass was definitely greener on the other side of the fence. The food was tastier too.

There'd be poached salmon with a delightful dill sauce for days!

ONE WEEK LATER, Kitty Bitteridge was being driven up a Connecticut country lane by Dimitri Kuznetsov.

They'd just attended a meeting in New York City.

A very important meeting.

Dimitri had also visited a bank to deposit the first money from the *America's Most Amazingly Talented Animals* grand prize. Sadly, the fine print stipulated that the "one million dollars" would be "payable in a financial annuity over forty years."

That meant Dimitri would only receive about twenty-five thousand dollars a year. And he would need to pay taxes on that.

"Cheaters," he muttered. "Liars . . ."

"Silence, Dimitri!" hissed Miss Bitteridge from the back of the stretch limousine. "By the time we're finished, you will be a multi-multimillionaire!"

"Let us hope so. Then even my chickens won't peck at my money."

"Is that another one of your folksy expressions I'll never understand?"

"Da!"

Miss Bitteridge smiled and stared out the window. Things had gone so well in New York City. The executives at the meeting were thoroughly convinced that Kitty Bitteridge was an unrivaled genius who could train any animal to do anything!

Because she was, and she could.

And, with time, her talents would be recognized and rewarded beyond the realm of show business. Because, truth be told, this was only the start. The start of something much, much bigger. She would move into the world of animal testing. What if animals willingly volunteered for drug, food, and cosmetics companies? What if they marched right into the labs and did whatever the humans wanted done? With her unique techniques, Kitty Bitteridge could make it look like the animals—cats, dogs, guinea pigs, whatever—were happily offering their services. Before long, she would rule that world too. The possibilities of this technology were endless. And it all belonged to her!

While she was plotting her next big thing, something caught her eye. A young girl at the side of the road. She was stapling a flyer to a telephone pole. A dog was with her.

"Dimitri?" Miss Bitteridge said. "Pull over. It's that girl from next door. Gabby. That dog is their Duke!"

Dimitri eased the long black car to a stop.

Miss Bitteridge powered down her tinted window.

"Hello, dear." She sounded as pleasant as she could pretend to be.

The girl and the dog turned to look at her. The girl held a stack of flyers and a staple gun.

"May I inquire as to why you are affixing sheets of paper to telephone poles?"

"One of our cats is missing," said the girl. She held up a Missing Cat poster. It showed a grayish cat with a grumpy, smooshed-in face. "His name is Mister Cookiepants."

The dog barked.

The girl nodded. "That's right, Fred. Mister Cookiepants has been missing for about a week. If you see him, can you please call this number?" She pointed to the phone number printed on the bottom of the poster.

"Of course, dear," said Miss Bitteridge. "Of course. Was Mister Cookiepants to be one of the stars of your new *Cat Flu* spin-off?"

"*Cat Crew,*" said the girl.

"Oh, right. Sorry."

"No. Mister Cookiepants wasn't interested in doing the show with us."

"He wasn't interested? My oh my. How could you tell?"

"You just can," the girl said with a shrug.

And, thought Kitty Bitteridge, *you can just make them interested in doing whatever you want them to do. That's*

*what animal training is all about! That's why the world
needs me!*

"Miss Bitteridge?" said the girl.

"Yes, Gabby?"

"It's Abby."

"Oh. My, what a lovely name."

"Anyway, I just wanted to say your cats were amazing on that TV talent show. How'd you get them to do all those tricks?"

Miss Bitteridge smiled a lipstick-curdling smile. "That's my little secret, dearie. Good luck on your quest to find Mister Cookieface."

"Cookie*pants*."

"Whatever."

Miss Bitteridge powered up her window.

"Drive, Dimitri. Drive!"

"Da."

The limo cruised down the road and pulled through the towering wrought iron gates of the Bitteridge estate, which swung open when Dimitri tapped a remote.

They pulled up the pebble driveway. The mansion loomed like a dark castle. Dimitri hopped out first so he could open Miss Bitteridge's door.

"Shall we go down to the gymnasium?" he inquired. "We have much work to do."

"In a minute, Dimitri. First I want to check in on our newest recruit."

She swept inside and headed to the library. She reached

toward a bookcase and grasped the spine of a hardcover first edition of *They All Saw a Cat*, tilting it downward. That section of the bookcase swung open to reveal a room with padded walls, several self-cleaning litter boxes, and sliding vents for automatic meal delivery.

On the floor, still as statues, sat eight Abyssinian kittens.

And one puffy gray cat with a smooshed-in face.

Every single one of them was wearing a collar.

"Hello, Mister Cookiepants," purred Miss Bitteridge. "It seems your friends next door are searching for you. Too bad they'll never find you!"

Miss Bitteridge tossed back her head to laugh maniacally.

And Mister Cookiepants kept staring blankly at the padded walls of his prison cell.

"JENNY?" SAID THE director. "Are you ready to shoot?"

"Ready!" Jenny shouted back.

She was with Fred, Mehitabel, Yakster, Barney, Clarence, and Squeak at the base of a fire escape that climbed seven stories to the building's roof. The whole production had moved up to Hartford, Connecticut, to film in the city's downtown district.

Abby's friend Zachary had tagged along to be an assistant on the camera crew.

Fred looked up and was glad that he only had to exchange a few lines with Mehitabel at the base of the first staircase.

Yes, Fred was still afraid of heights. Sure, when he pretended to be Duke he could also pretend he wasn't afraid of tall buildings or fire escapes or even the Eiffel Tower.

But given a choice, he'd rather just keep all four paws on the ground, thank you very much.

"You ready, Duke?" asked Jenny.

Fred gave her a hearty tail wag. This was it. They were actually going to film the final scenes for the first episode of the new show. With Nala's coaching and encouragement, both Clarence and Barney had become excellent additions to the feline cast. Yakster and Mehitabel were wonderfully nimble and athletic. And Squeak was so adorable, she was a natural scene-stealer. When Tater and Squeak were together, the "cute factor" was off the charts.

"Once we nail this scene," said Mehitabel, "our focus must shift to Einstein."

"It will," said Fred. "I promise. We're gonna save this show, the ranch, and your friend. We're gonna be one big happy family."

"Stand by!" called the director.

All Fred had to do for this final segment was wish Mehitabel good luck and watch her and her team storm up the fire escape with their ninja gear. They were on their way to take care of the notorious jewel thief known as the Pigeon. He was lurking up on the building's roof with his air force of real pigeons (also trained by Jenny).

"Is the cat cam ready to roll?" asked the director.

Zachary and another member of the camera crew came over to check the miniature harness-mounted camera that

Yakster was wearing. It would record the action from Yakster's point of view.

"Signal is five by five," said the camera tech. He tapped an On button. "We're rolling!"

"Quiet on the set!" shouted the director. "Roll all cameras. Aaaaaand . . . action!"

CAT CREW
EPISODE 1
"A FURMIDABLE NEW FELINE FORCE"
SCENE 22

No animals were harmed in the making of this film.® —Lily Morel, American Humane Film & TV Unit

THE EVIL JEWEL thief known as the Pigeon scuttles up the fire escape to the roof of the seven-story apartment building.

He holds up the dazzling jeweled collar he's just stolen off the neck of a kitten in a posh penthouse apartment. Its diamonds and rubies twinkle like stars.

"It's mine!" he says to the flock of pigeons cooing at him from their rooftop coop. "All mine! Karoo! Karoo!"

He picks up his poop gun—a Super Soaker loaded with gallons of gooey white pigeon glop. "If the police chase after me, I'll blast them!"

He coos with glee and, head jerking back and forth like he's pecking seeds, starts strapping on his jetpack.

Meanwhile, down on the street, Duke is with Tater and Mehitabel. The leader of the Cat Crew places a paw to the ear where she wears a miniature receiver.

"The Pigeon pinched Princess Squeak's collar!"

"Poor kid," says Tater. "She's had a ruff day. First the alien squirrels, now an evil supervillain jewel thief?"

Duke nods knowingly. "Yes, little buddy, it's a calamity!"

"Fear not," says Mehitabel. "When calamity calls . . ."

"Call in Cat Crew!" shout her crewmates Yakster, Clarence, and Barney.

"Guess it's time we headed upstairs to pluck a few pigeon feathers," says Mehitabel.

"Good luck!" Duke gives the cats a jaunty salute.

The four cats scamper up the nearby fire escape and race to the roof.

The music swells and the tension builds. It feels as if we're one of the brave warrior cats scaling the steep metal steps. We leap up the stairs, two at a time, and reach the rooftop in a flash.

"Freeze!" the Cat Crew shouts.

The pigeons take off, abandoning the diabolical jewel thief.

"Give us the collar," says Mehitabel. "Right meow."

"Ah, go lick yourselves!" scoffs the Pigeon. "You fur babies don't scare me!"

"Is that so?" says Yakster. "Well, maybe these will."

He flicks open both paws to show the Pigeon his hooked talons.

"Ninja claws at the ready, everybody!" commands Mehitabel.

All the cats shoot out their claws.

The Pigeon chuckles. "Save your claws for Santa. This collar is mine! Mine, I tell you!"

He presses the throttle trigger on his jetpack controls. Exhaust fumes spew out of the twin rockets. He rises an inch or two off the ground.

"Cat Crew? This is no longer a-mew-sing," says Mehitabel. "It's ninja time."

All four cats snap their paws open, and their detachable claws go twirling through the air like ninja stars! The razor-sharp weapons puncture the jetpack's twin rockets. Gas spews out from all sides. The Pigeon becomes a misguided missile. He whizzes and whirls around the rooftop like a balloon someone just set free.

He drops the sparkling collar.

Barney pounces on it.

The Pigeon crash-lands on his tail feathers.

"Ouch," says Clarence. "That had to hurt!"

"Yes," says Mehitabel. "I suspect the Pigeon is going to be feeling under the feather for a few days!"

The cats all purr and laugh and slap each other's paws.

The scene fades to black.

The episode ends.

And somewhere down below, a very happy Duke barks for joy.

FRED, SCRUFFY, AND NALA stood with Jenny, Abby, and Mr. Espinosa in the gravel driveway at the front of Jenny's house.

Fred was worried. They were waiting for the "big shots" from the network to arrive. It was time to show them *Cat Crew* episode one.

"It's not completely finished," said Scruffy. "They still have to tweak it and sweeten the track."

"I'm excited," said Fred. "I'm also nervous."

"Stop worrying about what can go wrong," suggested Nala, "and get excited about what can go right."

"I'm doing both!" said Fred. "If *Cat Crew* is a hit, Jenny can build all sorts of new dog kennels and cat cottages. Maybe even a new barn. She could rescue so many more animals. Our big happy family will be even bigger! But if it's a flop . . ."

Fred didn't have to go on.

Because Jenny was even more worried than he was.

"This is it, Leo," she said as a sleek sedan turned into the driveway. "If they don't love what we did . . ."

"They will, Aunt Jenny," said Abby.

Jenny grinned a little. "Oh, you can predict the future now too?"

"Abby's right," said Mr. Espinosa. "What's not to like?"

The car's doors opened. Four people dressed in business suits stepped out.

"Hi, guys!" said Jenny cheerfully.

"Welcome to the Second Chance Ranch!" chirped Abby.

Fred, Scruffy, and Nala wagged their tails in greeting.

"Jenny? Leo? Abby?" said a man in a suit. Fred recognized him from all the *Dog Squad* shoots. "This is Andrea. She's new to our team. She'll be in charge of *Cat Crew.*"

"*If* it fides a tibe slot od our schedule," said the woman named Andrea.

All of her *m*s sounded like *b*s, her *n*s like *d*s, because she was extremely congested. Her eyes were red and watery. Her stuffed nose was wet and runny. She was dabbing at both with tissues.

"Cad we please step idside?" asked Andrea. "I'b allergic."

"Oh dear," said Jenny. "To dogs?"

"Add cats."

"Here you go, Andrea," said another network lady, pulling some kind of nasal spray out of her suit coat pocket.

"Oh boy," said Scruffy as the people all trooped inside. "She's allergic to dogs *and* cats? This isn't good!"

"I need to wait right here," said Fred, sinking down to the ground.

"We'll wait with you," said Scruffy.

"Whatever happens," said Nala, "we can weather it better together."

"What are you three waiting for?" asked Mehitabel as she came trotting up the driveway.

"To find out our fate," said Fred with a heavy sigh.

"Aha," said Mehitabel. "This reminds me of that time when I was hidden inside a wooden horse outside the gates of Troy with my Greek friend Diomedes. We knew not what fate might await us. . . ."

Mehitabel regaled the dogs with her tale about the Trojan War for thirty full minutes. She finally reached the big finish.

"And that's why they say 'Beware of Greeks bearing gifts.' "

"Really?" said Scruffy. "Even if it's your birthday?"

Finally, the front door swung open.

All the people came rushing out to the porch. They were smiling! They were happy!

"Is that her?" said Andrea, the network executive with

all the allergies. She didn't sound stuffed up anymore. "Is that really Mehitabel?"

"Yes," said Jenny, with a laugh.

"She's clawsome!" said Andrea.

"Mehitabel says 'Thank you,' " said Abby, the pet psychic.

"Actually," said Mehitabel, "feelings of gratitude *were* flitting through my mind. . . ."

Andrea was so happy she clapped her hands at the dogs and Mehitabel. "Bravo, cast." She turned to Mr. Espinosa. "Can you have this episode ready to air a week from Friday?"

"Sure," he said. "No problem."

"Excellent. I'm giving *Cat Crew* the eight p.m. Eastern slot. That's prime family viewing time. And Leo?"

"Yes?"

"I want twenty-two fresh episodes, ASAP. *Cat Crew* is going to be a hit! A huge hit!"

THAT AFTERNOON, all the dogs and cats were treated to a feast on the lawn in front of the cat cottage.

There were tuna and salmon sashimi for all the cats. Filet mignon for Fred, Tater, and Scruffy. Nala had a homemade black bean veggie burger (with no onions or garlic).

"I wish Mister Cookiepants was still here," said Clarence. "He would've loved all this food!"

"Yeah," said Barney. "I'm so full, I'm like buttons on Santa's belly. I'm about to pop. If'n Mister Cookiepants knew what was waitin' for us when we was done shootin' this here show, he might not've run away like a dad-burned fool."

"Have you sent out a search-and-rescue party for the missing cat?" asked Nala. Search and rescue was her favorite kind of party.

Fred nodded. "Jenny and Abby have alerted the

authorities. They've also plastered Missing Cat posters all over town."

"The folks over at the Coastal Animal Shelter are on the lookout for him too," added Scruffy.

"Excuse me, canine friends," said Mehitabel, who had already finished her dinner and her post-dinner tongue bath.

"What's up, Mehitabel?" said Fred.

"Well, Fred, now that we've helped you and Jenny with *Cat Crew*, I was wondering if you three might lend your unique skills to a project that Yakster and I have put off for far too long."

"There's four of us!" said Tater.

"I'm afraid this is not a job for puppies," said Mehitabel, "no matter how eager and talented they might be."

"Oh. Okay. Squirrel! Gotta go!"

Tater took off after the squirrel.

"This endeavor I am about to propose could prove dangerous."

The three dogs leaned in closer.

"Dangerous is my middle name," said Scruffy.

"Really?" said Nala. "I thought your middle name was Fuzzface."

"Ah, that's just what Abby calls me sometimes."

"Please, Mehitabel," said Fred. "How can we help you?"

Mehitabel lowered her voice. "This is about those cats we saw at the talent show, Fred."

"They live next door," said Fred. "In Kitty Bitteridge's mansion."

"Indeed they do. Before we bunked with Charlie in the stable, Yakster and I observed one of their training sessions."

"They were incredible on TV," said Nala. "Even the goats at the yoga ranch were impressed."

"Yes," said Mehitabel. "They are all Abyssinians, one of the oldest breeds of domesticated cats. Direct descendants of the noble cats of ancient Egypt. When I myself was an Abyssinian in 2550 BC, we designed the Pyramids of Giza, scratching out our construction plans in the sand for the pharaohs."

"So that's why those cats are so darn good," said Scruffy.

"It's not the only reason." Mehitabel turned to where the kitten was soaking up the sun. "Squeak? Might you join us over here? It's time."

"Time for what?" asked Fred.

"For you dogs to learn the truth!"

"IT'S THE COLLAR!" screeched Squeak.

"Shhh," urged Mehitabel. "Not so loud. We don't want to panic Clarence or Barney."

"What about Yakster?" wondered Fred.

"He already knows. For we both witnessed it first-hand."

Fred turned to Squeak. "Tell us about the collars."

"They hurt," said Squeak. "If you don't do exactly what the humans tell you to do, you get a jolt!"

"Thank you, Squeak," said Mehitabel.

"You're not going to send me back to the mean lady, are you?"

"Of course not."

"Good. Because I like being Squeak. I hated being Kitten Number Nine!"

"You're safe now, little buddy," said Mehitabel.

"No harm shall befall you ever again," added Nala.

"Okay," peeped Squeak. "Cool."

She toddled off to her sunny napping spot.

"Poor kid," said Scruffy.

"Fortunately," said Mehitabel, "Squeak is a kitten. They live in the moment."

"It sounds like she was describing an electric-shock collar," said Nala.

"Indeed," said Mehitabel. "Fred, do you remember the collars the Swing Cats were wearing that night we were with the celebrity judges?"

"Sure." He gasped. "Those were shock collars?"

"Yes."

"I thought they were just for decoration."

Mehitabel shook her head and closed her eyes. "If only that were true, my friend. After enough jolts from those technologically advanced yet diabolical shock collars, the superintelligent Abyssinians become willing to do whatever their trainer or her evil henchperson asks them to do."

"This is horrible," said Nala.

"It gets worse," said Mehitabel. "One of our dearest friends, a nimble genius named Einstein, was trapped by Miss Bitteridge's evil assistant. Yakster and I have vowed to set him free, for he is our brother and he is in serious trouble."

Fred thought about what he might do if Scruffy or Nala or Tater or Reginald or any Second Chance Ranch creature was in danger.

He sat up straight. "Well, my friend, when trouble calls . . ."

He waited for Nala and Scruffy (or at least one of them) to fill in the blank.

They didn't.

"How many times do we gotta tell you, Fred?" said Scruffy. "That's on the show. In real life, we're just a bunch of pampered pooches."

"Speak for yourself, Scruffy," said Nala, stiffening her spine and matching Fred's heroic pose.

"All right, already," said Scruffy, striking his own courageous stance. "It's Dog Squad to the rescue."

"But first," said Fred, "we should go next door on a reconnaissance expedition."

"Oooh," said Scruffy, "like the time we spied on the mad king of Kantstandyastan and I had to crawl through that sewer and pop up in the gold-plated toilet of his royal throne room, which, hello, is what kings always call their bathrooms. That was a good episode!"

"And now that the first *Cat Crew* episode is a wrap," said Fred, "we're free for the rest of the day. I suggest the four of us slink next door and see what's going on."

"The five of us," said Yakster, who'd padded over to join the group. "Einstein is my brother too."

"We're glad to have you on the team, Yakster," said Fred.

"Just try not to be quite so chatty," suggested Scruffy. "It's a spy mission."

"Hey, like I said, I'm a Siamese. We're a very talkative breed. You might even say we're gabby. Verbose. *Loquacious* is a word I like to say even though I'm not exactly sure what it means, but—"

"Just don't do it when we are in our stealthy approach mode," said Mehitabel.

"Gotcha, boss. I can't argue with that. Coming in loud and clear. Roger, wilco. Aye, aye, Captain. Let's do this thing!"

42

FRED, NALA, AND SCRUFFY followed Mehitabel and Yakster as they made their way to the mansion next door.

"Their training facility is around back," whispered Mehitabel. "Follow me."

"Stick to the shadows of the trees," urged Nala.

"Watch out for security cameras and motion detectors," said Scruffy. "The evil villains always have 'em outside their nefarious lairs."

"It's true," said Fred, who had, of course, seen every episode of every season of *Dog Squad*.

Mehitabel shot up her right front paw to signal for everyone to freeze.

The three dogs stumbled to a stop and tumbled into each other.

"Sorry about that, Fred," said Scruffy. His snout was poking Fred in the butt.

"What's the problem?" Fred whispered.

"Scruffy was correct," said Mehitabel. "There is, indeed, a single-beam infrared security system ringing the perimeter of the house."

"Wow," said Scruffy. "You cats can see infrared beams?"

"No. But a little birdie told me about them."

"That's right," squawked a bird in a nearby tree. "My kids are sleeping up here. So don't you five furballs go triggering any alarms to wake 'em up!"

"Those black cylinders," said Yakster. "That's the receiver and transmitter. Or vicey versey. That one could be the transmitter, and that other one could be—"

"Shhh!" said the rest of the team.

"Right," whispered Yakster. "Gotcha. Roger that."

"Follow my lead," said Nala.

She pranced forward a few paces with her head angled to the right so she could stay focused on the precise location of the infrared receiver (or transmitter) on that side. Timing her movements perfectly, she sprang up and vaulted over where the beam would be.

Mehitabel and Yakster matched her moves, springing higher and leaping farther.

"Show-offs," muttered Scruffy. "My legs are too stubby to hop that invisible hurdle."

"I have long legs," said Fred. "Climb aboard, Scruffy."

Scruffy scrabbled up onto Fred.

"Give me a minute," Scruffy groused. "Need to get a good grip here. Hang on."

Finally, with Scruffy secure on his back, Fred trotted toward the unseeable security beam. When Fred reached the lift-off zone, Nala gave him a signal with her paw. Fred leapt. He cleared the undetectable barrier.

Fred made a soft landing. Scruffy jumped off his back. The whole team had safely thwarted the first layer of security.

Mehitabel and Yakster dropped to their bellies and crawled toward the narrow windows up ahead. Fred, Scruffy, and Nala mimicked their moves. They all wriggled forward until their wet noses were pressed up against the glass.

Fred peered down into a basement gymnasium filled with all sorts of training gear and quilted mats. The red-headed Kitty Bitteridge, wearing another dress with a cat pattern stamped all over it, stood with the Russian and another man in a frumpy business suit.

"Where are all the cats?" whispered Scruffy.

"The cats have arrived at the

studio," said the man in the flashy suit, as if he'd heard Scruffy's question.

"Excellent," said Miss Bitteridge, rubbing her hands together gleefully. She wasn't wearing the leopard-print gloves Fred remembered from the TV talent show. Her long nails were painted bright red to match the bright red of her lips. "Come, Dimitri. It's time. You must drive us down to the city. We don't want to be late."

The Russian man clicked his heels together and bowed slightly. "Da! It is our moment of triumph."

"One more thing," said the man in the suit.

"Yes, Mr. Teufel? What is it?"

"This training technique of yours."

Miss Bitteridge wiggled her red-tipped fingers. "You mean my Enhanced Electronic Method Of Obedience?"

"Exactly. Will EEMOO work with other animals?"

"We would have to make a few minor adjustments," said the Russian. "But da. It would work."

Mr. Teufel pressed on. "And is your system water-proof?"

"Why, whatever do you mean, Travis?" said Miss Bitteridge, coyly cocking up a penciled-in eyebrow.

"Would EEMOO operate if your subject was under-water?"

"Da," said the Russian. "With, as I say, minor modifications." He gestured toward a very large aquarium. It was filled with hundreds of gallons of water, but no fish.

"Something," said Miss Bitteridge, "that we anticipated you might request. So we took a few baby steps in that general direction."

"We are very proactive," said the Russian.

"Good, good," said Mr. Teufel. "Miss Bitteridge? Mr. Kuznetsov? Kindly block out your calendars for the next several months. I have a feeling the three of us are going to be very, very busy."

43

"WHERE'S YOUR FRIEND Einstein?" Fred whispered to Mehitabel.

"I suspect he is with the other members of the Swing Cats crew at the studio the man in the suit mentioned," Mehitabel whispered back. She was still squinting through the window, watching the three humans in the basement below. "Perhaps they are participating in another talent contest. Perhaps—"

Mehitabel gasped.

So did Nala when she saw what Mehitabel had already seen.

Fred's heart sank.

"Is that . . . ?" said Nala.

"Yes," said Mehitabel. "I'm afraid so."

"Wow," said Scruffy. "For a cat who ran away from home, Mister Cookiepants didn't get very far."

"Oh no," said Fred. "He's wearing one of the collars."

Mister Cookiepants stumbled across the floor on wobbly legs.

"Dimitri?" said Miss Bitteridge, her voice flinty. "What is that . . . *cat* . . . doing out of its containment area?"

"I am sorry, Miss Kitty. I must have failed to properly secure its chamber door. This is my fault, no one else's. I cannot blame a mirror for my ugly face."

Miss Bitteridge twirled her skirt and swooped across the room to the water tank. "Let's make the most of this interruption, shall we? Let's give Mr. Teufel a quick demonstration of the EEMOO's submersibility capabilities. Where are my gloves?"

"Coming!" Dimitri dashed over to a worktable and snapped open an aluminum attaché case with electrical cords plugged into its sides. "They are fully charged, Miss Kitty."

"Excellent. Excellent." She extended both her arms and wiggled her fingers impatiently.

Mr. Kuznetsov rushed over with the leopard-print gloves and helped her slip them on. He tugged up on the fur cuffs to make certain the fit was snug.

"We have electrode contact," he reported.

"Good. Good. And have we established a secure link to Mister Cookiepants's collar?"

"Da. The Bluetooth is engaged."

Miss Bitteridge made a quick circle with her right index finger.

The sleepy-eyed Mister Cookiepants, impossibly, executed a perfect backflip.

"Very good. Dunk him in the tank, Dimitri."

Mehitabel and Yakster gasped in horror.

"No!" said Mehitabel. "We cats hate water!"

"Steady, Mehitabel," said Fred. "Think about Einstein. Think about all those other brainwashed Abyssinians!"

"You're right, Fred," said Mehitabel reluctantly. "We mustn't blow our cover."

The Russian man plopped Mister Cookiepants into the massive water tank. Surprisingly, the floating cat didn't yowl or scratch or even hiss. Miss Bitteridge slowly waved her hands up and down like a hula dancer. The large cat swam gracefully, gliding back and forth across

the aquarium. Miss Bitteridge rotated one wrist and, instantly, Mister Cookiepants kicked off the side of the tank and started doing the backstroke.

"We need to tell Jenny about this!" said Fred.

"But how?" wondered Mehitabel.

"None of us speak Human," added Yakster.

"Abby!" said Fred, Nala, and Scruffy.

"Let's go!" said Fred.

He bolted away from the mansion.

Mehitabel, Yakster, and Scruffy took flight after him.

Nala was the only one who remembered.

"You guys?!?"

But it was too late.

A horn started blaring.

They had all hurtled through the infrared security beam and triggered the alarm.

MISS BITTERIDGE AND DIMITRI heard the alarm horns and darted to the basement windows.

They could see the tails of the trespassers fleeing across the lawn.

"It's those dogs!" hissed Kitty Bitteridge. "From next door."

"You mean Duke?" said Mr. Teufel. "From *Dog Squad*?"

"That's right," said Miss Bitteridge. There was a sly and malicious twinkle in her eye. "The Second Chance Ranch is just on the other side of those trees. Fortuitous, no?"

"Lucky, too," said Dimitri.

Mr. Teufel grinned a crooked grin. "You're the gift that keeps on giving, aren't you, Miss Kitty?"

"I try, Travis. I try."

"If something were to happen to Duke . . ."

She waved him off. "They'd probably go find another. Don't forget, this current canine crusader is actually a mutt named Fred. He replaced the original Duke when that Duke was injured."

Mr. Teufel tilted his head. Kitty could tell he was hatching some sort of wicked scheme.

"But," he said, "if Fred, I mean 'Duke,' were to, heaven forbid, perish in a very public way, surely the millions of loyal *Dog Squad* fans all around the globe would be shocked if his network attempted to quickly replace him after his untimely and, as I said, very public end."

"Yes," purred Miss Bitteridge. "You make a good point, Travis. That is definitely something to consider. Especially if certain other changes were already in place."

"I'm sure they will be, Kitty. You will soon be the most renowned animal trainer in the world! I suspect you'll need more trophy cases for all your awards!"

"Yes," said Miss Bitteridge as she imagined all the glory that would soon be hers. "I suspect I shall."

And with all those awards and accolades, it would be easy to move on to the next phase of her master plan. By the time she was done, she'd be far beyond awards and accolades. She would be a captain of industry! An animal-testing tycoon!

The businessman glanced at his phone. "More about what's next later. You two need to be down in New York City for the press conference. They just made the big announcement."

"How do I look?" Miss Bitteridge asked Dimitri.

"You are like a magnet," said Dimitri. "Very attractive."

"What about that swimming cat?" asked Mr. Teufel, gesturing toward Mister Cookiepants.

"Pull him out of the tank, Dimitri!" barked Miss Bitteridge. "Nobody likes a soggy cookie. Or wet pants!"

The three conniving villains tossed back their heads and laughed their fiendishly awful laughs.

FRED, SCRUFFY, NALA, Mehitabel, and Yakster burst into the main dog kennel at the Second Chance Ranch.

"Why're you guys panting so hard?" asked Dozer.

"Out . . . of . . . breath . . . ," said Scruffy.

"You should do like I do. You overheat, just drool and dribble."

"Have you seen Tater?" asked Fred.

"Sure," said Petunia. "He went for a walk with Abby and Zachary."

"Come on," said Fred. "They might be up at the house."

They bolted out of the kennel, reached Jenny's back door, scooted through the pet flap, and dashed into the TV room.

Abby was there, sitting on the couch. So were Zachary and Jenny and Mr. Espinosa. Tater was between Abby and Zachary.

All of them, including Tater, stared in wide-eyed disbelief at the screen.

"Um, what just happened in here?" muttered Scruffy.

"It sure doesn't look good," said Mehitabel.

Tater turned to the dogs and cats. "The TV just told us something bad, you guys. Real bad!"

Mr. Espinosa thumbed the remote. The image on the TV screen streaked backward.

Mr. Espinosa pressed another button.

The clip replayed.

Dramatic military music—a crisp drum and a bright bugle—filled the soundtrack as Kevin, the star of *Seal Team Seven,* tilted back his dive mask and spoke directly to the camera.

"Hiya, *Seal Team Seven* fans. Kevin here with some news you're gonna flipper out over! My new spin-off series, *Feline Force Five,* debuts tomorrow night, right here on the Big Hitz Network. I've teamed up with the amazingly clawsome cat crew formerly known as the Swing Cats."

The screen switched to footage from the Abyssinian drill team's performance on *America's Most Amazingly Talented Animals.*

"Every week, the Feline Force Five, with a little help from yours truly, will thwart supervillains like the Cat Burglar with their amazingly acrobatic ninja skills!"

Then the screen showed an action sequence from the show.

The ten Abyssinians were attacking a character dressed like a cat burglar on a rooftop filled with pigeon coops. They were hurling ninja stars, twirling nunchucks, and swirling swords.

"Feline Force?" barked Kevin, who was splashing around in a shallow rooftop puddle. "You cool cats definitely have my seal of approval!"

Animated graphics slashed across the screen.

"*Feline Force Five*!" said an offscreen announcer. "All new from the producers of *Seal Team Seven*. Premieres tomorrow night. Right here on Hitz!"

Fred was shocked. "They stole our show. *Feline Force Five* is just *Cat Crew* with seals instead of dogs."

Mr. Espinosa raised the remote and clicked off the video monitor.

Tater buried his head between his paws. He was trying to unsee what he'd just seen.

Finally, Abby spoke. "How'd Kevin the seal climb up to that roof?"

"Maybe he has a helicopter?" suggested Zachary. "But why do they call it *Feline Force Five*?"

"Yeah," said Abby. "I counted ten cats."

"They ripped off my ninja sequence," said Mr. Espinosa, sounding distant. "Someone leaked the script. We'll have to come up with a whole new ending. Maybe a whole new villain."

"They premiere tomorrow, Leo," said Jenny. Fred had never heard her sound so sad. "Tomorrow! You're talking about a major rewrite *and* reshoot."

"You think people will want to watch two different shows about crime-fighting cats?" Zachary asked innocently.

Abby dropped her head.

So did Jenny and Mr. Espinosa.

"No, Zachary," said Jenny. It was almost a whisper. "They probably won't."

And that was when the phone rang.

"THEY'RE KILLING *CAT CREW*," Jenny told the others after the call ended.

"What?" said Mr. Espinosa.

"The network's canceling our show."

"Before it even streams?"

Jenny nodded. "They agree with Zachary. Why would anybody want to watch two different shows about super-hero cats fighting supervillains?"

"Because our show will be better!" protested Leo.

"Sorry I said that thing about the two cat shows, Ms. Yen," said Zachary.

Jenny found a hint of her smile. "It's not your fault, Zachary. It's not anybody's fault."

"Oh yes it is," said Leo. "We have a spy on our crew. A mole! It's *their* fault!"

Abby looked like she might cry. "What's going to happen, Aunt Jenny?"

"I'm not sure. *Dog Squad* is in trouble too. Our ratings are down because of the seal show. We might have to cut back a little. Maybe help a few of our friends find new homes."

No!

Fred's worst fears were about to come true. He felt like he was teetering on the tip of the world's tallest building. His family was going to start splitting up and breaking apart.

Mr. Espinosa's phone buzzed. He looked at the screen.

"Aha! It's Sasha! The script supervisor!"

"What?" said Jenny.

"She just texted me her resignation. She's quitting *Cat Crew* and *Dog Squad* to 'pursue other opportunities.' Like selling us out to the folks at the Big Hitz Network."

"Come on, you guys," said Scruffy. "No way is Abby going to be able to read any minds right now. She's too upset."

The Big Hitz Network made some more news later that same evening.

Fred was with two dozen dogs in the main kennel. They were all gathered around a big-screen TV watching *Entertainment Nightly*.

"We like keeping up with the Hollywood buzz," Dozer explained to Fred.

"Oooh," said Petunia. "Check it out. News flash."

A BREAKING NEWS graphic slid across the bottom of the screen as the anchor read a news bulletin.

"This just in," said Caitlin Kelly, the anchor. "Miss Kitty Bitteridge, the genius animal trainer responsible for the amazing, cat-tastic antics of *Feline Force Five*, will also take over as trainer for the seven seals in *Seal Team Seven*."

The report switched to footage of the red-haired lady talking to a sea of news cameras.

"We're hoping to take Kevin and the gang to a whole new level," she told the reporters. "If you thought those seals did amazing stunts before, just wait until you see what they can do in my extremely capable hands."

She smiled and twiddled her fingers.

Her assistant, Dimitri Kuznetsov, told the reporters that "true success comes to him who builds something with the bricks others throw at him."

Fred remembered the talk they'd overheard about submersible shock collars. The experiment they'd witnessed with Mister Cookiepants in the water tank.

Kitty Bitteridge was going to "train" the *Seal Team Seven* seals the same monstrous way she trained her cats.

With electrical zaps and zings.

FEELING DOWN, Fred felt the need to apologize to each and every dog in the kennel.

"I'm sorry, Henry," he said to the basset hound, who looked like the saddest dog at the ranch. "Some of us might need to move to new homes."

He turned to the corgi Abby had adopted at the Coastal Animal Shelter's big charity gala.

"I'm sorry, Meatball."

"Yeah, me too," said Meatball. "I've enjoyed my time here."

"Best home I ever had," said Henry.

"Ah, there you are, old bean!" Reginald, the gorgeous golden retriever who starred in all sorts of TV commercials, strode into the crowded kennel. "I see you're still consorting with the common background players? You truly are a dog of the dogs, aren't you, Frederick?"

"These guys are my family."

"Yes, I'm sure they are. Listen, old boy—Jenny and I are rushing into production. It's a new commercial for our dear friends at YourHouse Real Estate."

"The ones where you open the door to the home of everybody's dreams?" said Fred.

"Correct. But in this new spot, after I, of course, open the front door, I am to scamper from room to room, ascend a staircase, and enter all the rooms on the second floor. They want me to wear a miniature collar-mounted camera. A doggy cam, if you will. I believe one of the cats in your ill-fated new show wore something similar as they ascended a fire escape?"

Fred nodded. "Yakster."

"Do you think he could tell me a little bit about it?"

"Sure. Yakster is very chatty. He'll tell you everything about anything, including that camera. It's very small. Smaller than my paw. And it records video on this teeny-tiny little computer card."

"My oh my. Sounds like a perfect device for one of your *Dog Squad* spy missions."

"Yeah," said Fred. "You could sneak in anywhere, record what the bad guys were doing, and then take the evidence to the proper authorities."

Fred froze.

He had an idea!

"Will you excuse me, Reginald? I need to go talk to the cats."

"Of course, of course. Kindly advise this Yakster fellow that I also wish to converse with him. Perhaps you might arrange a proper introduction?"

"You bet I will, Reggie. Right after I save the ranch!"

48

FRED SHOT OUT of the dog kennel and charged up the hill toward the cat cottage.

He was hatching a plan.

He'd wear the doggy cam. He'd record Kitty Bitteridge using her shock collars to train her cats.

After Fred had the footage he needed, he'd use the Tater-Abby connection to get the video evidence to Lily Morel, the American Humane observer who monitored all of Jenny's shoots. When Ms. Morel saw how Kitty Bitteridge treated her animals, the American Humane people would shut down *Feline Force Five*.

Cat Crew would be saved. No one would need to leave the ranch. Everything would be right again.

Maybe.

It was complicated, but it was worth a shot.

Fred rushed into the sunny room where Clarence,

Barney, Squeak, and Yakster were sitting in a circle listening to Mehitabel.

"And so, my feline friends, we must somehow rescue Mister Cookiepants *and* Einstein from the evil clutches of Miss Bitteridge."

"Don't worry!" said Fred. "I'm going to save Einstein, Mister Cookiepants, and all those other Abyssinians!"

"Really?" said Clarence. "Do tell us more."

Fred turned to Yakster. "I need that camera you had on your harness when you climbed up the fire escape."

"I don't have it," said Yakster. "A camera crew dude clipped it onto that harness Abby strapped me into."

"Okay," said Fred. "No worries. We just need to find the camera crew dude. And the camera. And—"

"Fred?" said Mehitabel.

"Yes?"

"What are you attempting to do?"

"Save *Cat Crew*. Save the ranch. Save your friend Einstein. Save Mister Cookiepants. Save all those who need saving!"

"Shoo-wee," said Barney, once again smacking a bottle cap as if it was a hockey puck. "That's a whole lot of savin' you're fixin' to do. You should open up a bank account."

Mehitabel looked concerned.

"Fred?"

"Yes, Mehitabel?"

"Remember that little birdie who told us about the infrared beam?"

"Sure. She was grouchy but helpful."

"Indeed. Well, she just flew to our windowsill and told us something new."

"What?"

"We won't let this happen, but . . ."

"But what?"

"Miss Bitteridge is plotting your demise."

"My what?"

"They want you—forgive my candid description—to have an unfortunate and, if possible, fatal accident."

Fred gulped. "Fatal?"

Mehitabel nodded solemnly. "I'm afraid so. Without you and your portrayal of Duke, there is no hope for *Cat Crew,* or even *Dog Squad,* continuing."

"The bird says they're putting up an electric fence," added Yakster. "Only it's not a fence. More like a net. And the wires are so thin, they're like a spiderweb. You won't even see the high-voltage trap until you've already walked into it."

"Well, Duke wouldn't let an electrified fence stop him from doing what needs to be done," Fred proclaimed. "When you're Duke, you just have to accept the risks that come with the job."

"Fred?" said Mehitabel. "You are not Duke."

Fred looked around desperately. He knew that

Mehitabel was right, but that didn't make it any easier to hear. "Well, I can sure try to—"

Mehitabel shook her head. "No one dog could ever possibly be the Duke we all know and love from *Dog Squad*. Duke is a fiction. A myth. A figment of Mr. Leo Espinosa's imagination. A marvel of green-screen technology and video tricks. A heroic ideal to strive for, perhaps, but an unobtainable goal nonetheless."

"What do you mean?"

"Simple: No one can save the world alone."

"But we have to stop Miss Kitty Bitteridge."

"Aha!" said Mehitabel. "Precisely!"

Fred was a little confused. "Precisely what?"

"*We* must stop her. We must work together. As I said, no individual can save the world. But working together? There's nothing we can't accomplish!"

Fred studied the faces of the cats who wanted to help him.

Cats!

He didn't have to be a hero all by himself.

He could be even more heroic if he let others help him handle the heroics.

"You are very wise," Fred said to Mehitabel.

She shrugged. "You live ninety-nine lives, you learn a few things. Now then, Fred—tell us your plan!"

Fred shook his head. "You mean *our* plan!"

"REMEMBER THAT LADY who was always on the set when we were filming *Cat Crew*?" Fred said to Mehitabel.

"Ah, yes," said Mehitabel. "Lily Morel. From the American Humane Film and TV Unit."

"That's right."

"I sat in her lap and purred a few times. I found her khakis to be quite cozy."

"Well," said Fred, "we need to tell *her* about Kitty Bitteridge."

Mehitabel nodded thoughtfully. "Indeed," she said. "For animals *will* be harmed in the making of the next *Feline Force Five* show. Ms. Morel will shut them down. And once the shock collars are removed, perhaps our friend Einstein will return to his normal, nonbrainwashed self. He will return to his family!"

"Exactly!" said Fred with an eager tail wag. "And

we can get Mister Cookiepants back to being himself, too!"

"Grumpy and grouchy?"

"Yep. Every family needs a sourpuss."

Mehitabel stroked her chin with a paw. "I see where you're going with this, Fred. We could use Abby's 'pet psychic' connection with Tater to communicate with Ms. Morel."

"She can read my thoughts too!" said Squeak.

"Oh boy," said Clarence, rolling his eyes. "Here we go again."

"It's true!" said Squeak. "The other day, I wanted a belly rub and guess what? Abby gave me one because she read my mind."

"Abby makes the quickest connections with puppies and kittens," said Fred.

"We will utilize both Squeak and Tater when the time comes," said Mehitabel.

"But is anybody gonna listen to them two young'uns?" said Barney. "Come on—they're just kids. Bean sprouts."

"People *will* listen," said Fred. "Because we're going to have solid proof. Video evidence! We'll go next door with that minicam Yakster wore for the fire escape scene. We'll catch Kitty Bitteridge in action and film her doing her dirty deeds."

"Yes!" cried Yakster. "Woo-hoo! Yowza!"

He raised a paw to slap a high five with Mehitabel.

But Mehitabel left him hanging.

"Alas," sighed Mehitabel, "going next door may prove difficult, if not impossible. As the little bird reported, the evil lady has installed invisible electrical fencing."

"If it's a fence," said Fred, "Nala can jump over it. Once she's safely on the far side, she can pull its plug."

Hope sparkled in Mehitabel's eyes.

"Very well. Let's gather up *all* our troops, combine the forces of the Dog Squad with those of the Cat Crew, and go on a scouting expedition to see exactly what we're up against."

"Good idea," said Fred.

Fred led the way to Scruffy and Nala's spacious doghouse, which they shared with Reginald.

"I'm in," said Nala after Fred told her the plan. "If the wire is six feet or under, I can clear it."

"She can," said Scruffy. "Anything higher? That's a little more iffy. Like that time you tried to leap over the clothesline, remember that?"

"Yes, Scruffy," said Nala, sounding slightly embarrassed. "I remember it."

Scruffy snorted back a laugh. "Came down wearing underpants on her head. Hi-larious!"

"And how might *I* be of assistance?" asked Reginald. "I'm up for anything. Except leaping. Or diving. I'd prefer not to do either of those. Actually, anything involving excessive exertion is a nonstarter for me."

"We might need your acting skills," Fred told Reginald. "After we know what we're up against. I have an idea about how to get the camera harness. You might need to pretend to be terrified of it."

"Jolly good!" said Reginald. "I do a marvelous petrified and panicked." He struck a trembling pose for a few seconds, then immediately snapped out of it.

"Hot dang," said Barney. "You looked like a scaredy-cat!"

"Acting is believing, my feline friend."

"Stand by for further instructions," Mehitabel told Reginald.

"Will do, madam. Good luck on your mission, chums!"

"Let's go!" said Fred.

The dogs and cats quickly reached Charlie's field.

Charlie went up on his hind legs and whickered as they approached.

"Hiya, Charlie," said Scruffy. "What's up?"

"Something's going on next door. Something bad."

"You sure?" said Scruffy.

"Yes. I heard the workers talking. It seems they're putting in a fence. A high-voltage security fence."

So the little bird had been correct.

Fred just hoped Nala could sail over whatever obstacle was waiting for them.

"THANKS FOR THE heads-up," said Fred.

"My pleasure," said Charlie. "And, if I might be of further assistance, please don't hesitate to ask."

"We won't," said Mehitabel.

The intrepid dog and cat team made their way through the trees and down to the babbling brook.

"Cats on backs," said Nala, orchestrating the crossing the way a good gym teacher might.

Mehitabel and Clarence climbed aboard Fred. Barney and Yakster scrabbled up to ride Nala. Scruffy was too short to ferry anybody.

"Let's move out!" barked Scruffy, splashing into the stream.

He doggy-paddled across.

When the entire team was on the far bank, they flopped to their bellies.

"I don't see any wires," said Fred, squinting hard.

"Doesn't mean they're not there," said Yakster. "You heard the horse. The wires are thin. Nearly invisible. We may never see them!"

"If only there were some way to gauge where they were," said Nala, "and how high they might be."

"Hang on," said Barney. "I'm fair to middlin' at boppin' bottle caps."

Fred nodded. He remembered trying to sleep in the cat cottage. Barney stayed up all night playing skittle pool with a plastic cap.

"I can shoot 'em up pretty high! See if there are any wires up there."

"But we don't have any bottle caps," whined Clarence.

"True," said Mehitabel, looking around, surveying her surroundings. "But we do have this handy pile of acorns!"

The four cats scrambled over to the heap of fallen nuts.

"Let's all try!" said Mehitabel.

She, Yakster, Barney, and Clarence started smacking, thwacking, and whacking acorns. The nutty pellets soared through the air until they hit something, maybe ten yards away, that made them spark.

"Aim higher, please," requested Nala.

The cats did.

Their chip shots sailed ten, twelve feet above the ground.

Still they sparked, sizzled, and exploded.

"It's too high," said Scruffy. "Nobody could leap over that electric force field."

Nala nodded. "I agree. Sorry, team."

"What about them long-tailed rodents, Nutty and Squiggy?" said Barney. "When it comes to trees, they're good at the scamperin' up *and* the scamperin' down."

Scruffy looked shocked. "The squirrels? They hardly ever talk to us. They have 'issues' with dogs. . . ."

"But Barney's right," said Fred. "Nutty and Squiggy could scramble up the tree and use its branches to make their way over the security fence."

"If," said Mehitabel, "the fence isn't even taller than the tree!"

51

"HANG ON A gol-dang minute," said Barney. "Need to fire one more test shot."

He gave an acorn a swift, sideways scoop shot with a lot of lift.

The nut flew just below the tree's extended branches and landed safely on the far side of the unseen electric fencing. No sizzle. No explosion.

"All righty," said Barney. "Them branches are above the electrified fence."

"I'll go fetch Nutty and Squiggy," said Fred.

He raced back to the hutch where the squirrels lived with a few rabbits (they did Easter candy commercials).

Nutty and Squiggy quickly agreed to their mission because they quickly agreed to any kind of climbing and scampering requests. They'd actually completed their light-footed dash through the treetops to the mansion and back by the time Fred rejoined the cats and dogs on the far side of the stream.

"They're gone," said Nutty.

"Long gone," said Squiggy.

Nutty nodded. "Will be for the next few days."

"Well, Nala," said Scruffy, "looks like you don't need to pull the plug no more."

Nala nodded. "And I was so looking forward to it."

"I wonder where everybody went?" mused Mehitabel.

"Oceanside Amusement Park," said Nutty and Squiggy.

"How could you two possibly know that?" scoffed Clarence.

"A little birdie told us," said Nutty.

"We scooched through her tree," added Squiggy. "She heard the humans talking earlier."

Nutty picked up the report. "They're gonna be filming the next episode of *Feline Force Five* up the road at the amusement park. Shooting starts at six a.m. tomorrow."

"Wow," said Yakster. "That little bird talks even more than me and I talk a lot, know what I mean, huh, huh?"

"Yes," droned Clarence. "We know."

"Thanks, you guys," Fred told the two squirrels.

"Anybody eatin' them acorns there?" asked Squiggy with a nod to the pile.

"Nope," said Barney. "We was just usin' 'em to shoot chip shots up and over the invisible fence yonder way."

"Seriously?" said Nutty. "You animals were playing with your food?"

"There's enough there for a whole winter," said Squiggy. "Well, at least through January."

"Have at them, gentlemen," said Mehitabel. "Fred? We need to, pardon my pun, nut out a new plan."

"I SEE, OLD CHAP," Reginald said to Fred. "I am to act terrified of the camera harness and insist that before I wear it for my commercial shoot, they strap it on *you* for a full twenty-four hours so I can observe how it operates."

"Exactly," said Fred.

"Quite a convoluted request, wouldn't you agree?"

"We're sorry, Reginald," said Mehitabel. "But it's the best we can do at the moment."

"Better a diamond with a flaw than a pebble without," said Nala.

"Very well," said Reginald. "Since you put it that way . . ."

"Hang on," said Fred. "Here comes Scruffy with Tater and Squeak."

"Oh my," said Reginald. "I have to work with children?"

"They both have a special connection with Abby."

"Yes," said Reginald dryly. "I'm sure they do."

"Aha," said Mehitabel, spying something over near the barn. "And here comes Abby with the young Babkow boy."

"Let's go!" said Scruffy. "Time for Reginald to make his demands known to management!"

"Just Fred, Reginald, Tater, and Squeak should chat with Abby," said Mehitabel. "It would seem peculiar if we all swarmed over there at once."

All the dogs and cats nodded in agreement.

Abby and Zachary sat down on a bench in front of the big red building's side door.

Fred (with Squeak clinging to his head), Tater, and Reginald trotted across the open field. As they drew closer, Fred could hear Abby and Zachary's conversation.

"We'll probably have to find new homes for some of the dogs," said Abby. "The cats, too. And Charlie. The horse."

"Wow," said Zachary. "I'm so sorry."

Abby sighed. "Reginald's doing a commercial next week. That'll help some. . . ."

"Hey, check it out," said Zachary, pointing at Fred. "There's a cat riding on Duke's head."

Abby turned to look.

"And Reggie?" whispered Fred. "You're on!"

"I refuse to do it!" Reggie whined. "I'm afraid of harnesses!"

All Abby and Zachary heard were the whines and whimpers. But they instantly understood that Reginald was miserable. Abby sprang up from her seat and knelt in front of him. She took his head in her hands.

"What's wrong, Reggie?" Abby asked.

"He's upset!" shouted Tater. "About wearing the harness."

"What harness?" said Abby.

"The one with the camera!" barked Fred.

"The one with the camera," repeated Squeak.

"What's going on?" said Zachary, who, unlike Abby, wasn't a pet psychic.

"I think Reginald is upset about the camera harness we want him to wear at that commercial shoot," Abby explained.

"Yes!" whooped Reginald, Fred, Tater, and Squeak.

"He'd be more comfortable with it if I wore it first!" said Fred. "For one whole day."

Tater and Squeak passed on the message.

Abby raised her hands to her temples.

"Are you getting something?" asked Zachary.

"Yes. An idea." She lowered her hands and started gently rubbing Reginald's ears. "Hey, big guy, how about if Fred wore the harness for a day? What if he showed you it's no big deal?"

"Mmmmm," said Reginald, enjoying his ear massage. "Lovely."

"He says that'd be lovely!" reported Tater.

"But," said Fred, "he wants to see me carrying the full rig. The camera has to be loaded up with everything that'll be used in the shoot. Battery, video card, the works."

Squeak and Tater took turns relaying all that information, but Abby understood.

"We need to make sure Fred has all the camera gear, too," said Abby.

"No problem," said Zachary. "I know how to hook it up."

"You do?" said Abby.

Zachary shrugged. "I'm thinking about getting into film when I go to college. Guenther, the director of photography, has been mentoring me. He even showed me how the cat cam rig worked when Yakster wore it for the fire escape scene."

"Awesome!" said Abby. "Come on, Fred. Let's head over to the camera truck. Reginald? Don't worry. Fred's going to show you there's nothing to it."

"Easy-peasy," Fred said to Reginald with a wink.

"Yes," said Reginald. "That certainly was."

53

THIRTY MINUTES LATER, Fred had a small camera clipped to his collar.

"According to Zachary," Fred reported, "this camera has hypersmooth video stabilization, it's waterproof,

and it can record up to one hundred minutes of picture and sound on a fully charged battery."

"Hang on," said Scruffy. "How will Ms. Morel and the American Humane people be able to watch whatever you record?"

"Easy," said Fred. "They'll just pop out the SD card."

"SD?" said Nala.

"Secure digital," said Fred. "That Zachary? When it comes to camera gear, he's a total geek."

"Good for him," said Mehitabel.

The Joint Dog and Cat Strike Team—a name that Yakster had come up with—was assembled in the cat cottage. To make sure Jenny and Abby didn't get suspicious, Fred, Nala, Reginald, and Scruffy would soon return to their doghouses for their supper and standard after-dinner nap.

"We'll sneak out of our bungalows and regroup at Charlie's barn at midnight," said Fred, gesturing toward the swinging-tail cat clock hanging on the cottage wall. "I'm sure Kitty Bitteridge will be working with those poor cats bright and early tomorrow morning at the amusement park."

"How far away is this park?" asked Clarence.

"We went there once," said Nala. "For the grand opening of the merry-go-round. Remember, Scruffy?"

"Oh yeah. All them horses bobbing up and down and goin' nowhere except back to the starting line."

"It's only about three miles up Route One," Nala continued.

"No problem," said Mehitabel. "Cats can walk five to ten miles in a single day. I suggest we stick to the trees and underbrush lining the side of the road. We don't want any of the Romans to see us on the march."

"Romans?" said Reginald, arching an eyebrow.

"Sorry. I was remembering the sneak attack I went on with Hannibal when we crossed the Alps to sack Rome."

"They had elephants," added Yakster.

"Indeed we did. But on this quest? We will have only each other!"

"Might I ask another question?" said Reginald.

"Please do," said Mehitabel.

"This one isn't about Romans. Or elephants. It's about buttons." He turned to Fred. "How do you intend to turn that camera on, dear boy? As I'm sure you're already aware, you don't have fingers. And your limbs aren't flexible enough for you to tap it with your front paw."

"I know," said Fred. "I'm going to need help. Mehitabel? Will you do the honors? When the time comes, will you bop the camera's On button?"

"It will be my pleasure."

"Thanks. Unfortunately, we won't be able to eject the video card."

"So what're we gonna do?" gasped Yakster. "If the American Humane people can't see the video, this whole plan is a waste of time."

"We'll use the Squeak-Tater-Abby connection again," said Fred. "If that doesn't work, we can claw the camera off the collar and drop it into their laps. Lily Morel will be on the set with Reginald when he films his real estate commercial."

"Marvelous plan," said Reginald. "Marvelous indeed. However, I believe my part is now concluded. As Fred mentioned, I'll be filming a commercial. Therefore, I need my beauty rest. I shan't be joining you at midnight."

"We thank you for all you have done for the cause," said Mehitabel, bowing graciously. "More importantly, Einstein and Mister Cookiepants will thank you when the camera you helped us obtain secures their freedom!"

A LITTLE AFTER midnight, the Joint Dog and Cat Strike Team regrouped at Charlie's barn.

Fred was still wearing the camera. He and Mehitabel rehearsed the paw swat that would power it on.

"We are good to go," said Fred.

"Your cause is just," said Charlie. "Your plan solid, if complex. I wish I could aid you in its execution."

"Don't worry, Charlie," said Scruffy. "We've got three dogs and four cats. We aren't horsin' around."

Charlie whinnied politely at the weak pun but quickly turned serious. "How will you navigate in the dark?"

"The cats will take the lead," said Mehitabel. "We can see twice as well as dogs at night."

"I wish you well," said Charlie. "It's good to have you all working together as a team."

"Time's a-wastin', folks," said Barney. "We need to

hike on up to the amusement park without gettin' lost like a fart in a fan factory."

Fred turned to Mehitabel. "Did he just say . . ."

"Yes," she replied. "I'm afraid he did. Follow me, everybody!"

As planned, they scooted through the foliage lining Route 1 and headed north. While they rambled through the brush, Fred thought about Mister Cookiepants. And Einstein. And all the other zombie cats from the talent show.

He was also a little worried about Kitty Bitteridge. She was out to get him. Everybody said so. Was he walking into some kind of trap?

Two and a half hours (and one very long-winded story from Yakster about the time he met a turtle) later, the Joint Dog and Cat Strike Team arrived at the currently closed Oceanside Amusement Park.

The moon slipped out from behind the clouds, illuminating the towering skeletal outlines of the roller coaster, Ferris wheel, and parachute drop.

"The gates are locked," said Fred.

"That's never stopped an alley cat," said Mehitabel. "There is always another way."

"Found it!" called Yakster, who'd scuttled off to examine the park's chain link fence for weak spots. "There's a bashed-in break near the bottom of this panel. You dogs just need to dig out a little dirt, make a trench, and we're all sliding into the park, free of charge!"

Fred and Nala, who had the longest and strongest legs, went to work scooping up the soft and sandy soil.

In no time, the whole team was on the other side of the barrier.

"There!" said Nala, pointing at some tents and RVs over near the park's giant Ferris wheel. "That's a film company's base camp if ever I've seen one."

"And we've seen dozens!" said Scruffy.

"Let's prowl closer," suggested Mehitabel. "But might I suggest we do it on cat paws?"

"No can do," said Scruffy. "I'm a dog."

"She means we should approach very, very quietly," said Yakster.

Barney turned to the three dogs. "Y'all need to be quieter than a mouse peein' on cotton."

Fred turned to Mehitabel again.

"Yes," said Mehitabel. "He really said that, too."

The team moved closer to the tents and trailers.

Suddenly, they heard a voice.

With a thick Russian accent.

"Miss Kitty, we are going to need much more power to control all these cats and Kevin the seal!"

Fred and the others dropped to their bellies. Now they could see the silhouettes of Miss Kitty Bitteridge and her curly-haired henchman, Dimitri Kuznetsov.

"Kevin has much insulating blubber," grumbled Dimitri. "His collar must be amped up. And that Abyssinian I snatched from the alley? He is not obeying commands as speedily as he should."

"Einstein," whispered Mehitabel. "He's a fighter!"

"I can't wait to meet him," Fred whispered back.

"And then there is Mister Cookiepants," said Dimitri, jabbing a thumb over his shoulder to indicate one of the trailers. "There are too many animals to control with battery packs. We need another source of power!"

"So find it!" hissed Miss Bitteridge. "The park will be closed to the public tomorrow. We can use all the power we want."

"This is good," said Dimitri. He held up a thick electrical cable. "Request permission to siphon electricity from Ferris wheel."

"Permission granted!"

Dimitri saluted and jammed the blunt end of the cable into a junction box. Fred heard a sizzle.

"We have very much power now, Miss Kitty," said Dimitri.

"Yes," purred the evil cat woman, twiddling her fingers menacingly. "We do! Soon, every animal on earth will do my bidding! Soon they will all bow down to me! I will control them all! Mwah-hah-ha!"

THE JOINT DOG and Cat Strike Force Team spent the rest of the early morning behind a dumpster in one of the amusement park's service alleys.

Although there would be no paying customers coming to the park, the Ferris wheel started to turn at sunrise. And, judging from the distant calliope music, so did the merry-go-round.

The dogs and cats waited patiently for Miss Bitteridge to start "training" her cats. From their hiding place, they could see everything that went on in the area where *Feline Force Five* had set up its home base.

Finally, Kitty Bitteridge and Dimitri Kuznetsov appeared. They hauled cat carriers from a trailer and stacked them in an open paved area behind one of the tents.

"This will be our final rehearsal before we begin shooting," said Miss Bitteridge. "We have several hours until the rest of the crew arrives. Including, of course, our new and highly paid script supervisor."

Kuznetsov chuckled. "Sasha was a very good spy, stealing the *Cat Crew* script. She is someone I could share a bowl of borscht with on a cold Siberian night."

"Bop the button," Fred whispered to Mehitabel.

"Bopping!" She smacked the camera's power switch with her paw. It was now recording everything Miss Bitteridge and Mr. Kuznetsov did and said.

"Do we have sufficient voltage, Dimitri?" said Miss Bitteridge.

"Da. With all the extra electricity from the Ferris wheel, the shock collars will be packing quite a punch."

"Let's make certain, shall we? Give me Number Ten."

Mr. Kuznetsov opened a door on one of the crates. Miss Bitteridge wriggled her hands into her leopard-print gloves. The Russian man fiddled with the collar on the cat they called Number Ten. Fred heard the familiar ripping sound of Velcro being adjusted.

"That's Einstein!" gasped Yakster.

"Shhh!" said Mehitabel.

"Give me the cat with the smooshed-in face, too!" Miss Bitteridge commanded Kuznetsov.

"Coming right up."

Fred heard more Velcro snapping.

"That's Mister Cookiepants," gulped Clarence.

"All set," Mr. Kuznetsov said to his boss. "Your wish is their command."

"Wonderful." She flicked up her right hand.

Mister Cookiepants yelped and jerked out his legs. The fur on his back shot straight up.

Fred had seen and heard enough. Someone needed to stand up for Einstein and Mister Cookiepants and all the animals unfortunate enough to end up with Miss Kitty Bitteridge. He made sure the camera was pointed in the right direction to capture all the despicable deeds being done by the evil animal trainers.

Miss Bitteridge waved her gloved hand up and down.

Mister Cookiepants wiggled his butt.

"Excellent!" Miss Bitteridge clapped with glee.

The clapping gestures made Mister Cookiepants do a strange, bobble-headed shuffle.

"Remove the test subject," Miss Bitteridge shouted at Kuznetsov. "It is time to try our turbocharged collars on the most stubborn Abyssinian of them all. Number Ten!"

"Da," said Dimitri.

He grabbed the dazed Mister Cookiepants by the scruff of the neck and tossed him into one of the trailers. Then he marched over to a control box and twisted some dials. "Try now with Number Ten."

Miss Bitteridge twiddled her gloved fingers.

Einstein stood on his hind legs and began to dance.

Miss Bitteridge snapped up her right index finger.

Einstein performed a backflip.

She spread open the fingers on her left hand.

Einstein did a split.

"There you have it," Mehitabel whispered to Fred. "Proof positive that she isn't 'training' her cats. She's torturing them!"

A new figure stepped out of a second production trailer. Mr. Travis Teufel. The network executive. He was wearing the same frumpy gray suit.

"Is Kevin the seal responding to *his* collar? Will we be able to speed up production on *Seal Team Seven* as you promised, Miss Bitteridge?"

"Definitely." She turned to Kuznetsov. "Have you fitted and fine-tuned Kevin's collar?"

"Da. He is in the pool inside the tent. We test it now?"

"Yes, Dimitri. We test it now." She rubbed her gloved hands together. When she did, Einstein performed a shimmy shake. "Switch my glove link to seal frequency one."

"Switching link," said Mr. Kuznetsov, flipping up a lever.

"You will soon see what a genius I am, Mr. Teufel," boasted Miss Bitteridge.

"Great. And then I want you to do a quick interview with Caitlin Kelly from *Entertainment Nightly*."

"Is she here?"

"Yeah. The marketing team set up an exclusive behind-the-scenes package. Caitlin is waiting over by the Ferris wheel."

"Fine," said Miss Bitteridge. "We'll give you a quick

demonstration with Kevin. Then I will happily chat with Ms. Kelly!"

The three chuckling villains marched toward the production tent.

Fred prowled forward on his belly.

"Whoa," said Scruffy. "Where do you think you're going?"

"I'm going to follow them," said Fred. "We should capture footage of them using their 'training techniques' on Kevin, the star of *Seal Team Seven*."

"A capital idea," said Mehitabel. "But I'm going with you."

"Us too," said Nala.

"Yeah," said Yakster. "We're all going. We're a team. It's what teams do. Like in baseball. You don't just send a pitcher out to the mound. You need nine players. I think. Maybe eleven. No, wait. That's football."

"Yakster?" said Mehitabel, shaking her head.

"Riiiiight. The camera's still picking up everything I say, right? Not that any of the humans would understand it. Just a bunch of meows to them. But maybe I should just stop talking. Yeah. That might work."

Fred smiled. "And so might this plan. We just need this one last piece of evidence. Come on. Let's go *seal* the deal!"

THE TEAM SILENTLY crept toward the tent.

They couldn't see what was going on inside, but they could hear water splashing and the angry honk of seal barks.

"Catch him, Dimitri!" they heard Miss Bitteridge shout. "Loop that rope around his neck!"

"Dang," said Barney with a gulp. "They're gonna strangle that poor flipper flapper!"

Mehitabel attempted to calm him. "Most likely they are simply using a Ketch-All animal control pole with a loop at the end to make Kevin the seal easier to handle."

Fred nodded. "That's how I was captured the last time I wound up in an animal shelter. I better do this part alone."

"Agreed," said Mehitabel. "If we all appear in the tent entrance at the same instant it will certainly draw their attention. Crawl in, grab a few seconds of footage, and crawl back out. Our mission here will be complete."

Fred dropped to his belly and scooched along the ground. He quietly worked his way into the tent.

But there was a big wooden equipment crate blocking his view. So he sidled stealthily to the right.

When he did, he could see the star of *Seal Team Seven* sitting in a shallow aboveground pool, maybe ten feet wide and one foot deep. Kevin looked dazed. Numb. He looked miserable.

Unfortunately, Miss Bitteridge wasn't doing anything for Fred's spy camera. She was just standing there, with her hands on her hips, waiting for the Russian man to finish tightening the Velcro strap of Kevin's control collar.

Mr. Teufel was holding the four-foot-long aluminum pole with the loop at the end—the device they'd used to catch Kevin and bring him under control.

"Are we ready, Dimitri?" Miss Bitteridge asked impatiently.

"Da!" said the Russian, stepping back from the shallow pool.

This is it, thought Fred. *This is the money shot!*

Miss Bitteridge fluttered her fingers. Kevin grimaced and went through a series of odd and unusual moves.

"You see, Mr. Teufel, it's all in the gloves. Dimitri designed the prototype of this device for his cat act back in Moscow."

"Da," said Dimitri. "Is true. Too bad the Russian authorities called it barbaric. Pah, I say to them. Pah!"

"My finger movements tell the collar when to shock

236

the performer. I remove the jolt when the performer does as I desire."

Fred heard Kevin whimper.

"Have you ever seen a seal dance the chicken dance, Mr. Teufel?" Miss Bitteridge asked gleefully. "Kevin will now show you how it is done!"

She twitched and twisted her gloved fingers.

Kevin danced the dance.

"All of your seals will gladly do my bidding, Mr. Teufel! They will do my bidding or, like my cats, they will suffer the consequences. Mwah-hah-ha!!!"

Fred felt like he was going to be sick.

This was too much.

These bad people were like all the bullies in the world who thought they could push weaker creatures around. Thank goodness he'd joined forces with Mehitabel and the Cat Crew. Together, they were stronger than any of them could be on their own. Together, they could even stand up to a monster like Kitty Bitteridge!

"Okay, okay, Kitty," said Mr. Teufel. "I get the picture. You're even tougher on Blubber Boy than our current trainer!"

Fred had the picture too. Enough video evidence to show the American Humane people and the world. He scooted around to make his exit.

But he was crawling out of the tent just as someone else was walking in.

He looked up.

It was Caitlin Kelly. The reporter from *Entertainment*

Nightly. Not too long ago, Fred and Jenny had done an interview with her to promote *Dog Squad* when Fred took over the lead role.

"Well, hello, Duke!" she said with a laugh. She leaned down to pat Fred on the head. "What're you doing back here? Spying on the competition?"

Fred sat up and smiled a queasy smile. He nervously wagged his tail.

Suddenly, he felt the looped end of an animal control pole around his neck.

He turned his head and saw Kitty Bitteridge. She tightened the rope and handed the pole to Dimitri.

"Hello, Caitlin," said Bitteridge. "My next-door neighbor, Jenny Yen, will be so grateful when I tell her we found her Duke. Apparently, he ran away from home this morning."

"Oh dear," said the TV reporter.

Miss Bitteridge nodded knowingly. "Between you and me, those *Dog Squad* dogs aren't very well trained. They deserve better than what Jenny can offer them."

"Well," said Ms. Kelly, "that's why I'm here. Thought I'd try to get a sneak backstage peek at *your* training techniques."

"Sorry," said Miss Bitteridge. "My methods must be kept confidential. I'm sure you understand."

"Of course. But you can't blame me for trying."

"No," said Miss Bitteridge, crinkling her ruby-red lips with a forced smile. "I suppose I can't."

FRED FELT HORRIBLE.

For one thing, he'd been caught. The American Humane people might never see the video he'd captured with the spy camera. Without it, how would they know they had to free all the animals being abused by Kitty Bitteridge and her henchman?

For another thing, Miss Bitteridge was saying terrible stuff about Jenny. Ruining her reputation. Making the TV lady think Jenny was the bad trainer.

"We have Duke now," said the Russian man, tightening the rope around Fred's neck ever so slightly. "He is safe."

"Thank goodness," said the reporter.

Fred felt the earth quake. Overhead he heard a rattling rumble.

"Ah," said the man in the suit. "Right on schedule. They've started up the Runaway Mine Train roller coaster for us. The log flume ride as well. Those will be our first shots this morning. Kevin will be in the splashdown pool, waiting for the cats sliding down the chute in a log. He will send Feline Force Five chasing after the evil villain known as Train Wreck, who'll be on the roller coaster. Should be a great action sequence."

"Yes," said Miss Bitteridge. "In fact, Caitlin, you might want to set up your camera over by the log flume. We'll work with Kevin first. Then we can sit down and do our interview."

"Perfect. And the cats will actually ride the log flume ride?"

"Oh yes," said Miss Bitteridge, with a flutter of her gloved hands. "My Abyssinians will do whatever I ask of them."

"Awesome."

"I'll escort you onto the set, Ms. Kelly," said Mr. Teufel.

"I'll call Jenny," said Miss Bitteridge with a smile that looked like it hurt. "She'll be so happy to hear that we found her number one star!"

Mr. Teufel led the reporter out of the tent.

The roller coaster rattled by overhead again.

Miss Bitteridge waited a moment, then raced to the tent's entrance. She looked left. She looked right.

"Good. They're gone!"

Phew, thought Fred. *She didn't see Mehitabel and the others. They must've found a new hiding place.*

"This is our lucky break, Dimitri!"

"Da?"

"This is our chance to give Duke the very public end we were hoping for. And *Entertainment Nightly* is here to report the tragedy to the world."

"Go on. Tell me more."

Miss Bitteridge held up her gloved hands to frame a scene only she could see.

"In a fit of jealousy, Duke, also known as Fred, escaped from the Second Chance Ranch and dashed to the Oceanside Amusement Park so he could attack the stars of *Feline Force Five*. When he saw the cats rehearsing in the roller coaster, he went chasing after it. Sadly, a second train came barreling down the tracks and crashed into him, sending Fred flying to his untimely demise!"

The Russian nodded. "This might work. We need to position him on the tracks in a spot where no one can see what we are up to."

Miss Bitteridge's eyes widened. "The tunnel! The roller coaster screams through a dark mine shaft after its final turn. No one will see what we're doing back there. Fred will be a goner. So will *Cat Crew* and *Dog Squad*! And Jenny Yen! I alone will be the world's most renowned animal trainer. There will be no one to stop me! Mwah-hah-ha!"

Now the Russian was practically giddy. "You really are a genius, Miss Kitty!"

"Yes. I know. I am."

She leaned down to give Fred the creepiest head pat he'd ever felt in his life. It made him shiver.

"And what have we here?" said Miss Bitteridge, finally noticing the miniature camera mounted on Fred's collar.

"Is dog cam," said the Russian. "To give dog-eye point of view for action scenes."

Miss Bitteridge snapped the camera out of its holder.

"He probably ran away from wherever they were shooting yesterday," she said. "The camera department will be looking for this. Too bad they'll never find it." She tucked it into her cat purse and zipped it shut.

NOOOOO!

Fred's heart sank.

All the evidence of Kitty Bitteridge's animal cruelty was on a memory card in that camera. Now she had it. And the world would never see it.

"Miss Kitty?" said the Russian. "Why do you think this dog is really here?"

Miss Bitteridge gave Fred another chilling look. "Because Fred is a very clever and cunning boy, isn't he? First he stole the lead role in *Dog Squad* from the original Duke. Now he is here to sabotage *Feline Force Five* and *Seal Team Seven*."

"This is true? A dog can plot and scheme like that?"

"Only when they're as ambitious and ruthless as Fred. After all, he lives in a dog-eat-dog world. Don't you, Fred?"

Fred actually snarled. The evil lady was so wrong. He

didn't care about fame and glory. He'd done what he'd done to help other animals. To set them free.

Right now, he couldn't care less about starring in any television shows. He just wanted to save Einstein, Mister Cookiepants, Kevin the seal, and all the Abyssinian zombie cats being controlled by Kitty Bitteridge and her shock collars.

He had to stand up for all the underdogs. He couldn't let the bad guys win. Not today. Not ever! It wasn't just what Duke would do. It was what Fred had to do!

"Quickly, Dimitri. Slip a control collar around Fred's neck. We'll want him to walk into that roller coaster tunnel all by himself." She twiddled her fingers. "But he might need a little . . . encouragement!"

FRED DIDN'T KNOW what to do.

He had no plan.

No hope.

The Russian strapped one of the electronic collars around his neck. When Fred attempted a quick sidestep, he felt a tingling jolt shoot through his body.

"Keep walking, dog," commanded the Russian. "We go to the roller coaster."

Fred heard one empty train click-clacking its way up the first steep hill as another whipped around the turns. At the far side of the coaster, there was a rickety wooden tunnel, built to resemble a ramshackle mine shaft. The screech of the steel wheels echoed off its walls as the coaster plunged into darkness.

"Are the Abyssinian cats secure?" asked Miss Bitteridge.

"Da. They are all wearing their collars and obeying

your 'sit and stay' command in the holding area behind the tent."

"Excellent. What about the cat with the smooshed-in face? What about Mister Cookiepants?"

"He is wearing his collar and sleeping in the trailer. Kevin the seal is sleeping in his kiddy pool. In short, all our animals are currently under control. We are free to take care of Fred at our leisure."

"Good. Good."

"We should scoot under these girders," said the Russian. "There is a hidden set of access steps on the far side for amusement park maintenance workers."

Fred kept walking. He didn't want to feel another jolt to his neck.

He tried to think of some kind of heroic action he could take to escape.

What would Duke do?

Easy. Duke would karate-chop his kidnappers. He'd lasso them with his leash. Then he'd blast off in his jetpack.

Except Duke never had a shock collar strapped around his neck. And Fred didn't have a leash or a jetpack. He wasn't very good at karate, either.

Fred finally understood what Mehitabel had been trying to tell him all along: No one can save the world alone. Heck, Fred couldn't even save *himself* by himself.

"This way," grunted the Russian man, grabbing the collar to drag Fred up a set of wooden steps.

Fred dug in his paws.

"Bad dog!" shouted Miss Bitteridge.

ZAP!

"Bad, bad, bad dog!"

ZAP-ZAP-ZAP.

Fred felt woozy. Like he might pass out. Like his brain would turn to mush if he didn't do something fast.

But he couldn't do anything except the one thing he knew he had to do.

"HELP!" he called out. "HELP! HELP! HELP!"

FRED'S YELPS EARNED him more jarring jolts.

His legs went rubbery.

But in the distance he heard a familiar voice.

"Fred's in trouble!" shouted Scruffy.

"It's a calamity!" screeched Yakster.

"When trouble calls," shouted Nala, "it's Dog Squad to the rescue!"

"And," cried Mehitabel, "when calamity calls, call in Cat Crew!"

Fred's eyes were bleary.

But he could see Nala and Scruffy charging toward him. Mehitabel, Yakster, Clarence, and Barney, too.

"Who are these foul creatures?" hissed Kitty Bitter-idge.

"My friends!" wheezed Fred.

That earned him yet another punishing shock.

He had to shake his head to clear his eyes. Because now he was seeing things that couldn't possibly be there!

Two squirrels hanging on to a horse being led by a golden retriever with a little birdie on his back, all trailed by three dozen other barking dogs!

61

"HANG ON, FRED," shouted Mehitabel. "We'll get that collar off you in a flash."

Fred heard something rip as the clever cat used her paws and claws to make a series of very precise swings, slashes, and swats.

"Got it!" shouted Yakster, snatching up the collar with his mouth as if it was a cat toy. "I'm dumpin' this thing in the nearest trash bin!"

Meanwhile, Nala and Scruffy led the charge of the dog brigade. Fred's furious friends snarled at Kitty Bitteridge and her flunky, Dimitri. Fred saw Dozer and Petunia and Meatball and Henry and Izzy and Waffles and Dolce and Teddy and—everybody!

"We need her purse!" Fred shouted as best he could. "She took the camera. We need her gloves, too. They control everything!"

"On it!" screeched Nutty and Squiggy. The squirrels

leapt off Charlie's back and joined the mad dash of dogs chasing the evil animal trainers across the amusement park toward the nearby merry-go-round.

The little bird swooped down and fluttered in the air.

"Aerial reconnaissance mission complete," she chirped to Mehitabel.

"Report?" said Mehitabel, sounding like the field general of an army. (She'd probably spent one of her ninety-nine lives with Napoléon.)

"The ten Abyssinians, including your pal Einstein, are over by that tent. Kevin the seal's inside, flopping around in a wading pool."

"Any sign of Mister Cookiepants?" asked Barney.

"Yeah, I saw him waddling around in the parking lot," reported the little bird.

Mehitabel turned to her formidable feline force. "Cats? Claws at the ready. We have more Velcro collars to tear off!"

"We're gonna rescue Kevin the seal!" gushed Clarence, sounding excited. "I've always wanted to meet him. I LOVE *Seal Team Seven*. Sorry, Fred, but I do!"

Fred actually laughed. "That's okay, Clarence," he said. "I love that show too."

"Come on, y'all!" cried Barney. "Let's go rescue Mister Cookiepants."

"Give him my best," Fred shouted to Barney. "Hurry, Mehitabel. Take your Cat Crew and free them all. I'm gonna help everybody chasing after Kitty Bitteridge."

"I'll stay here with Reginald," said Charlie. "I'm too old for chase scenes."

"I'll be right here with you, noble friend," said Reginald. "I'm too well groomed for chase scenes."

Fred dashed off. The pack of Second Chance Ranch dogs chased Miss Bitteridge and Dimitri around and around the merry-go-round. The squirrels scampered across its canopied roof.

"Attack!" shrieked Nutty.

He and Squiggy went flying for Miss Bitteridge. They landed on top of her head. Their clawed feet snagged her blazing-red hair.

"Rodents!" she screeched. "Airborne rodents!"

She swung at them hard with her purse. So hard, the purse went flying.

Nala chased after it. Six other dogs chased after Nala.

"Dimitri?" squealed Miss Bitteridge. "Get these filthy rats off me!"

"I can't!" he screamed back as he danced a jig. "The dogs are nipping at my ankles!"

Suddenly, Mehitabel came charging across the midway, followed by her Cat Crew and the ten freed Abyssinians.

"Stand back, everyone," bellowed Mehitabel. "The new Cat Crew has arrived. We'll take it from here!"

FRED WATCHED IN stunned amazement as more than a dozen cats scrambled up and down Kitty Bitteridge as if she was a carpeted climbing tree.

The evil animal trainer peeled off her leopard-print gloves and flung them to the ground so her hands were free to swat and claw at the cats.

"Get off me! I command you!"

She wiggled and waggled her fingers. She waved her hands.

But she wasn't wearing her controller gloves.

And the cats weren't wearing their shock collars.

Miss Bitteridge dropped to the ground and shielded her head with both her arms.

Mr. Kuznetsov tumbled down to the asphalt too. He rolled into a ball. "Don't hurt me! Please don't hurt me!"

"Cats?" declared Mehitabel. "Stand down. The enemy has surrendered!"

The cats sprang back and joined the dog pack to form a tight circle around the two cowering animal trainers.

"I got the purse!" said Nala, trotting over.

"I got it open," said Petunia the Doberman.

"She ripped the thing to pieces," said Dozer. "She shredded it!"

Petunia shrugged. "We're all good at different things."

"So true," said Reginald, leading Charlie over to join the circle of friends penning in the two nefarious villains.

"Thanks for coming, everybody!" said Fred. "I definitely needed all your help!"

"I agree," said Charlie. "It's why Reginald and I organized the march from the ranch to the amusement park—an hour after you folks set out. We figured you might need backup."

"We hid over there," said Reginald, pointing to a ride called the Tunnel of Love.

Suddenly, there was a loud THWUMP.

It was followed by a ZIZZ and a ZUNK.

The Ferris wheel's lights went out.

It stopped turning.

"Ooops," said Scruffy, loping back to join the group. "I think I did that. I tossed Miss Kitty's electronic controller gloves into the log flume ride. They sizzled when they hit the water. I think they might've also short-circuited somethin'."

"They were drawing their power from the Ferris

wheel," said Yakster. "Remember? We heard them talking about it."

"Yeah," said Scruffy. "I remember. Now. Kind of forgot about it when I tossed the gloves into the water."

"Hey, where's Mister Cookiepants?" said Barney.

"I ripped off his collar," said Clarence. "Then I went to rescue Kevin."

"Did Mister Cookiepants follow you?" said Fred.

"Nope. The second he snapped out of his trance, he went looking for something to eat."

Fred heard a screech of tires.

Now what?

JENNY AND ABBY came racing into the amusement park in their pet transport van.

They both practically leapt out of the cab.

"Perfect," said Fred when he saw the puppy and kitten in Abby's arms. "Abby brought Tater and Squeak!"

"You're all here!" said Jenny, sounding relieved.

"I had a dream that you all were in trouble!" said Abby. She lowered Squeak and Tater so she could hug Fred, then Nala, then every other dog and cat within hugging distance. "There was a roller coaster in my dream."

"What on earth is going on?" shouted Mr. Teufel, the network executive. He tromped over to the merry-go-round to see what all the ruckus was about. He was trailed by Caitlin Kelly and her *Entertainment Nightly* camera crew.

"These hideous creatures are assaulting me!" sniffled Kitty Bitteridge.

"They ripped the cuffs of my tuxedo pants!" added Dimitri.

"I'm sure they had a good reason to do it," said Jenny.

"Ms. Yen? I'm Travis Teufel from the Big Hitz Network, home of *Seal Team Seven* and, starting tonight, *Feline Force Five.*"

He said it like Jenny should be impressed.

She wasn't. "I know who you are, Mr. Teufel."

Caitlin Kelly gestured to her camera operator. He propped his rig on his shoulder and started shooting. The reporter jabbed her microphone toward Mr. Teufel and Jenny.

"Are you attempting to sabotage our shoot?" Teufel demanded.

"She is!" said the disheveled Kitty Bitteridge. "That's exactly what she's doing! Sabotage!"

"Why are all my animals here?" asked Jenny.

"Because you sicced your dogs and cats on us," claimed Dimitri.

"Ha!" said Jenny.

While the humans bickered, Squeak and Tater bounded over to where Mehitabel and Fred stood in the circle ringing the two animal trainers.

"What's going on, Fred?" asked Tater.

"Yeah," added Squeak. "How come everybody ran away from home?"

"We were on a mission," said Fred.

"To save our friends," said Mehitabel.

"I knew you'd come back for me," said the Abyssinian standing beside Mehitabel.

"Of course, Einstein. We're family. And families stick together, through thick and thin, feast or famine."

"We couldn't let her torture you like that," added Yakster. "Or any of those other cats. But first we had to star in a TV show so we could learn about search-and-rescue missions and then team up with all these dogs and those squirrels and that horse. The little bird wasn't part of the original plan but, hey, she proved very helpful. Chatty, too. Extremely talkative, know what I mean?"

"Tater?" said Fred. "Squeak? We need you two to communicate with Abby. That box on the ground near Nala is a camera. We captured everything on video! Jenny and Abby need to see it, right now. Hopefully, they'll share the footage with Lily Morel from the American Humane TV and Film Unit. They need to share it with whoever can help shut down Miss Bitteridge and her cruel and unusual training techniques."

"Wow," said Squeak. "That's a long message. Too many characters."

"That's okay," said Tater. "We can handle it. Because nothin's too ruff for us."

Tater and Squeak scampered over to where Abby and Jenny were still arguing with the lady in the cat dress, the man with the curly hair, and the other man in the business suit.

"Your dogs and cats attacked me!" shouted Miss Bitteridge. "You have absolutely no control over them!"

Jenny grinned. She turned to the dogs and cats, shook her head, and said, "You guys?"

That was all it took.

The dogs sat. So did the cats. Even the ten Abyssinians.

There was no more snarling or hissing.

Which was a good thing. Because Tater and Squeak had an urgent message to communicate.

"Hey, Abby?" barked Tater.

"Yo, Abby?" peeped Squeak.

"Check out that camera over near Nala!" said Tater.

"Yeah, check it out!" added Squeak.

Abby had a puzzled look on her face.

"The camera, the camera, the camera," shrieked Squeak.

"Nala, Nala, Nala!" said Tater.

"Aunt Jenny?" said Abby.

"Yes, hon?"

"Fred was wearing the camera rig this whole time. He was showing Reginald there's nothing to be afraid of."

"Not that I was actually afraid of it," Reginald whispered up to Charlie.

"Of course not," the horse whispered back.

Abby pointed at Nala. "Nala's got the camera that was mounted on the collar. If they found a way to switch it on . . ."

"We did," said Mehitabel.

"Which," Abby said with a squint, "I think they did, we might be able to see exactly what happened."

"Bingo," said Scruffy. "It's showtime."

Nala picked up the camera, pranced over, and placed it at Abby's feet.

"I think we should look at whatever is on its video card," said Abby, placing her hands to her temples. "I think we should look at it right now."

"I've got a laptop!" offered the reporter.

Yes! thought Fred.

The dogs all smiled and panted. The cats purred and meowed.

Now it was Miss Bitteridge, Mr. Kuznetsov, and Mr. Teufel who were doing the snarling and hissing.

"No! We were filmed without permission! You'll be hearing from our lawyers!"

Jenny ignored them.

She picked up the camera and handed it to the TV reporter. "Here you go, Caitlin. If Fred and the gang captured anything interesting, *Entertainment Nightly* can run it first."

THIRTY MINUTES LATER, while the search continued for Mister Cookiepants, *Entertainment Nightly* broke a story headlined FELINE FORCE FIVE USES TERRIBLE TRAINING TECHNIQUES.

Sixty minutes later, Lily Morel from American Humane appeared on several different cable news networks to proclaim that "many animals were harmed in the making of that TV show! The same might be true for *Seal Team Seven*!"

The Big Hitz Network canceled the world premiere of *Feline Force Five,* which had originally been slated for that very night.

Seal Team Seven was put on "a long-term hiatus."

The network also fired Mr. Travis Teufel and encouraged "all our rightly disappointed animal-loving viewers to catch *Cat Crew* when it premieres next week."

The Connecticut State Police, accompanied by representatives of the ASPCA, arrested Miss Kitty Bitteridge and Mr. Dimitri Kuznetsov for animal cruelty. The ASPCA also helped the Coastal Animal Shelter rescue the eight other Abyssinian kittens caged in the Bitteridge mansion.

Jenny volunteered to foster all the animals that had been held captive by her neighbor. She shuttled the dogs and cats and squirrels back to the Second Chance Ranch, keeping an eye out for Mister Cookiepants.

"He's probably napping somewhere sunny," said Jenny. "We won't leave until we find him."

The bird arranged her own transportation. Mr. Babkow drove over with his pickup truck and Charlie's horse trailer.

Fred and Mehitabel stayed with Abby at the amusement park. They both wanted to make sure everyone else was safely transported before they rode the last shuttle home.

"We should continue our search for Mister Cookiepants," said Mehitabel. "But first, let me thank you most sincerely for helping us save our dear brother Einstein."

"Thank *you*, Mehitabel," said Fred. "You helped me save my home. No, wait. You helped *us* save *our* home!"

Mehitabel sighed. "The Second Chance Ranch isn't

truly our home, Fred. As much as Yakster and I have enjoyed our time at Jenny's place, we are—and always will be—alley cats."

"That's not true. You weren't an alley cat when you built the Pyramids or rode inside the Trojan horse or lived at the White House with Abraham Lincoln."

Mehitabel considered that. "True. You make a valid point."

"So, stay with us. *Cat Crew* is going to be a smash hit. I can tell. And Jenny will work your pal Einstein into the cast. Any of the other Abyssinians who want to stay and play can live with us too!"

Mehitabel nodded thoughtfully. "You have given us much to think about, Fred. And think about it we shall."

Abby came over to where Mehitabel and Fred sat waiting.

"Aunt Jenny called. She's on her way back with the van."

Abby looked around the empty amusement park. "But we still can't find Mister Cookiepants."

"Yoo-hoo!" came a voice from somewhere up high. "Meow!"

Fred, Mehitabel, and Abby craned their necks and looked up to the top of the Ferris wheel.

Mister Cookiepants was poking his head out of the highest car.

"Need a little help!"

Fred's stomach was a little jittery. The girders of the Ferris wheel reminded him of the Eiffel Tower. Mister Cookiepants was soooooo high above the ground.

"Hang on," said Mehitabel. "I'll come get you."

"No," said Fred, taking in a deep, fortifying breath. "*We'll* do it."

Abby was about to dial 911 and summon the fire department when Mehitabel and Fred scampered off to the Ferris wheel.

"You guys?" said Abby. "What do you think you're doing?"

"Working together, of course," said Fred.

"Yes," added Mehitabel, "as I've often said before: If you want to go fast, go alone. If you want to go far, go together!"

And maybe Abby understood.

Because she put away her phone and watched in awe as the dog and the cat leapt from car to car and clambered up to the top of the frozen Ferris wheel.

When they reached Mister Cookiepants, Mehitabel helped him climb onto Fred's back and grip the camera collar he was still wearing.

"Wow!" said Mister Cookiepants, hanging on for dear life. "We're up so high!"

"Really?" joked Fred. "I hadn't noticed."

He and Mehitabel laughed.
And then they all climbed back down.
Together.

THANK YOU TO THE
CAT CREW CREW!

First and foremost, thank you to my wife, J.J. Grabenstein (coauthor of *Shine!*), who, twenty-some years ago,
turned this "cats stink" dog lover into a cat fanatic who
often writes with a kitty in his lap.

Thanks to Shana Corey, my longtime editor at Random House. She's like an excellent stage director, seeing
what you've done well and showing you where you might
do better. Thanks also to Polo Orozco, assistant editor.

Extra-special thanks to Beth Hughes, the amazing art-
ist of the cover and all the illustrations sprinkled through-
out the book.

Thanks to all my other friends at Random House
Children's Books who have done so much for my books,
especially John Adamo, Shameiza Aly, Barbara Bakowski,
Michelle Cunningham, Tia Resham Cheema, Kathleen
Dunn, Janet Foley, Lili Feinberg, Kate Keating, Alison
Kolani, Barbara Marcus, Kelly McGauley, Shaughnessy
Miller, Michelle Nagler, Janine Perez, Kristin Schulz,

Erica Stone, Tim Terhune, Jen Valero, Rebecca Vitkus, April Ward, and Adrienne Waintraub.

Thank you to my literary agents, Carrie Hannigan and Josh Getzler, and the whole dogged squad at HG Literary.

And finally, thank you to all of you who made adoption your first option by rescuing dogs and cats and giving them the one thing they can never give themselves: a loving furever home.

DISCOVER HOW IT ALL BEGAN. . . .

Go back to start and meet young Luigi Lemoncello BEFORE he was the world's favorite game maker, when he was just an ordinary kid who liked to spin the dice!

A *NEW YORK TIMES* BESTSELLING SERIES

"Discover the coolest library in the world." —JAMES PATTERSON

★ "A worthy successor to the original madman puzzle-master himself, Willy Wonka." —*BOOKLIST*, STARRED REVIEW

Is it fun? Hello! It's a Lemoncello!

TURN THE PAGE FOR A SNEAK PEEK AT *MR. LEMONCELLO'S VERY FIRST GAME.*

It was the summer that changed Luigi L. Lemoncello's life.

Which, of course, led to millions of other lives being changed. The events of that long-ago summer gave rise to families made closer by games played late into the night or on rainy vacation days. It also ushered in a magical factory, a spectacularly futuristic library, dazzling contests, an unquenchable quest for knowledge, stupendous surprises, and fantastic fun unlike any the world had ever seen or experienced.

But we're getting ahead of ourselves.

In 1968, Luigi had just turned thirteen. He was the sixth of the ten Lemoncello children. His older brothers and sisters were all super-serious, super-talented, straight-A students. Luigi, on the other hand, loved making up stories. He loved solving puzzles. And he really, really loved playing games.

Everyone said he was, well, different. Maybe even peculiar. Definitely odd.

On weekends, Luigi's father ran the projector at the Willoughby Bijou Theater on Main Street in Alexandriaville, Ohio. Whenever there was a Saturday matinee for kids, Mr. Lemoncello would sneak his children up to the projection booth with him.

It was the only way the whole family could afford to see movies.

For free.

The Lemoncello kids would take turns peering through the small window next to the clacking movie projector. They'd each watch for a few minutes and then tell their brothers and sisters what had happened.

"The millionaire was boxing with the bad guy," Luigi said after his turn at the window.

And then he added his own spin.

"That's when a kangaroo hopped into the ring!" he told his brothers and sisters.

"A kangaroo?" exclaimed the youngest Lemoncello, Sofia.

"Oh yes. And the kangaroo can really sing!"

Luigi's sixteen-year-old brother, Fabio, motioned for Luigi to step aside. "It's my turn. You're being goofy."

"No," said Sofia. "Let Luigi go again. He tells the best movies."

But Fabio wasn't about to give up his turn.

"Okay, now the guy who loves cars is singing a song about Detroit. . . ."

Luigi pressed his ear to the wall.

"DEE-TROIT! DEE-TROIT! DEEEEEEE-WOOOOO-WAAAA-TA-TA-TA-TA . . ."

The movie soundtrack warbled to a stop.

The Lemoncello kids, their eyes wide, swiveled to face their father.

"The projector's jammed," said Luigi's father with a frustrated sigh. "I told Mr. Willoughby we should replace this clunker. Stand back, everybody. I need to make a splice."

Mr. Lemoncello was very handy and could fix almost anything. He flicked up some light switches, shut down the clattering mechanical monster, and pulled both ends of the filmstrip out of its feed sprockets.

While his father wrestled with the two enormous film reels, Luigi heard the audience downstairs. They were chanting and stomping their feet.

"We want the movie!"

"We want the movie!"

Kids hurled boxes of popcorn. Sugar Babies and Sno-Caps bounced around the auditorium like spitballs.

"Go down and tell them about the singing kangaroo," Sofia urged Luigi.

"Huh?"

Luigi was used to telling his family stories. And his friends. Sometimes the kids at school.

But an auditorium filled with strangers?

"Go," said Sofia. "Hurry!"

"No!" hissed Luigi's oldest sister (and harshest critic), Mary. "Don't you dare embarrass us."

The crowd below was chanting louder. Their foot stomps became a thundering herd of cattle. Mr. Lemoncello was nimble and quick with his hands, but he needed more time.

"We want the movie!"

"We want the movie!"

Luigi looked over to Sofia.

She smiled. "You can do it!"

Luigi raced down the steep staircase from the projection booth, tore across the lobby, and slammed through the swinging double doors into the auditorium.

The theater was dim, but Luigi saw a soft circle of light pooling on the empty screen.

He ran down the center aisle.

Took a deep breath.

And stepped into the faint spotlight.

This was soooo different from telling his little sister a funny story. He could barely see kids in the seats, just their hazy silhouettes.

"Um, good afternoon, boys and girls," he began.

The kid shapes squirmed. They seemed annoyed or bored or both.

Luigi looked up to the projection booth. Sofia was in the window, smiling down at him.

He had to do . . . something.

"Uh, I bet you're all wondering what happens next!"

"Yeah!" yelled a voice from the darkness.

"Well, um, as they drive to Detroit, a big wind kicks up, and all of a sudden their car can fly—just like in *The Absent-Minded Professor*! They sail through the clouds and—"

THUNK! SPLAT!

A half-empty Pepsi cup smacked Luigi in the face. Sticky brown syrup dribbled down his nose.

"Sit down, weirdo," shouted a blond boy in the middle of the auditorium. He looked to be about fifteen.

The girl next to him squirmed in her seat. "Leave the kid alone, Chad."

Luigi figured he had two choices. He could run away, or he could stay and try to change the story he was suddenly starring in. Maybe even make it funny.

"Now, then," he said, comically wiping his face the way he'd seen the Three Stooges do after being clobbered by banana cream pies. "Where was I?"

"Blocking the screen!" shouted the guy named Chad. "Who do you think you are, anyhow?"

Good question, thought Luigi. Who was he?

"Uh, nobody, really."

"Well, do you know who *I* am?"

"The Mad Pepsi Bomber?"

The crowd laughed.

"No, weirdo. I'm Chad Chiltington. And my best friend

is Jimmy Willoughby. His old man owns this movie theater. How'd you sneak in here? You don't look like you could afford to buy a ticket. I'm going to report you to Mr. Willoughby!"

Uh-oh! thought Luigi. If Chad Chiltington did that, Luigi's father could lose his projectionist job.

"I'm sorry. I was just trying to—"

Suddenly, light flickered on the screen, warbly music slid up to speed, and the movie started. His dad had saved the day. The kids in the auditorium cheered. Chad Chiltington draped his arm over his girlfriend's shoulders. He also snagged her Pepsi cup, since he didn't have one anymore.

He had forgotten all about Luigi Lemoncello.

Well, Luigi sure hoped he had.

The Lemoncello family was so huge, they ate dinner every night the way some families do on Thanksgiving or Christmas.

With two tables.

Luigi's mother, father, and five older brothers and sisters sat at the big table. Luigi sat with his four youngest siblings at a fold-up card table. Stromboli, the cat, slept on the sideboard. Fusilli, the dog, sat patiently under the smaller "kids' table," because the younger Lemoncellos dropped the most food.

It had been a week since the incident at the movie theater.

Luckily, nothing bad had happened. Mr. Lemoncello still had his projectionist job. Luigi hadn't been barred for life from the movie theater. Nobody had thrown another half-empty cup at him. Even scowling Mary seemed to have forgotten it.

The Lemoncello family lived in a cramped apartment building at 21 Poplar Lane in what was called the Little Italy section of Alexandriaville. Most of their neighbors were Italian. Or Irish. Or Polish. The Italians had arrived first, so the crowded cluster of four-story brownstone buildings was named after them.

"Here you go, guys," said Luigi, pulling three hand-drawn cards out of an envelope. He placed them side by side on the kids' table. "It's a new game. I just invented it."

"What is it?" asked Alberto, who was eight.

"A secret code!" said Luigi.

"Neat," said ten-year-old Arianna.

"Cool," said Massimo, who was the second youngest, at six.

The first card showed a dog. The second, an orange. A goat was on the third. Luigi tapped the three cards, one at a time.

"In this game, you have to figure out what I'm spelling by using the first letters of the pictures. For instance, this is how you'd spell 'dog.' *D-O-G.*"

Five-year-old Sofia had a puzzled expression on her face.

"Why do you need all those cards to spell 'dog'?" she asked. "The first one has a dog on it."

The big table erupted with laughter. Luigi's older brothers and sisters were all watching.

"Always with the games," said the oldest, eighteen-year-old Tomasso.

"You should spend more time studying!" said Mary, who was the next oldest, at seventeen. "Make something out of yourself. Quit being such an oddball."

Luigi had heard this before. Many, many times. Most of his brothers and sisters already knew what they wanted to do when they grew up. Fabio was going to be a lawyer. His teachers had been telling him since kindergarten that he'd make a good one.

Francesca, on the other hand, would become a doctor. A brain surgeon. She was only fifteen but had already figured out her whole life.

"What're you going to do, Luigi?" asked Lucrezia, who was only one year older than Luigi. "Waste your time playing games?"

"Break another window?" said Tomasso, shaking his head.

"Maybe shatter some more mirrors?" added Mary.

Ugh, thought Luigi. *Nobody's ever going to forget that.*

Last winter, during a blizzard, when everyone had been stuck inside the cramped apartment, Luigi had had an idea for a game.

It included a golf ball.

And a slingshot.

When it was Alberto's turn, he went for a toilet-bowl plunk-and-plop.

Unfortunately, Alberto ricocheted his shot off the medicine cabinet (shattering the mirror) and out the bathroom window (shattering *that* glass too).

Mr. Lemoncello, who was extremely clever, tacked up an old woolen blanket and a sheet of cardboard to block out the gusting winter wind. He also worked out a payment plan with the landlord to have the window and the medicine-cabinet mirror replaced.

And even though it had been Alberto who actually broke the mirror and window, everyone knew the truth.

It was all Luigi's fault.

He picked up his handmade game cards and slid them back into the envelope.

Soon steaming bowls of food, with wheels on their bottoms, rolled around the table on the train-track device Mr. Lemoncello had engineered to make serving dinner to twelve hungry people faster. Everyone forgot about Luigi and his First Letters game.

Everybody except Luigi.

"Did you hear?" said Lucrezia. "The Poliseis are going to Florida for vacation!"

"We should go to Florida!" grumbled Arianna.

"Your father would need to *get* a vacation first," said Mrs. Lemoncello. "And Mr. Willoughby doesn't believe in them. Neither does the Belkin Bicycle Factory."

Mr. Lemoncello glanced at his watch. He had three different jobs. The seven-to-three shift at the bicycle factory. Night janitor at the big department store downtown. And weekend work at the movie theater. None of them gave him a vacation or paid enough for a trip to Florida.

Luigi sometimes felt it was his fault that his dad had to work so hard. After all, he was the one always breaking things that cost money to replace. He was the one who wasn't going to grow up to be a fancy doctor or lawyer. Maybe Luigi needed to get his head out of the clouds.

"There's a reason most people only dream at night," Mary often reminded him. "Bad things happen when you do it during the day!"

When he finished changing his clothes after church the next day, Luigi bolted out the back door of his apartment building to meet his two best friends.

Bruno Depinna and Chester Raymo were both thirteen, like Luigi. They were waiting for him in the crackled asphalt alleyway that was their hangout.

Luigi had a mop of curly black hair, black eyes, and what some people called olive skin, even though Luigi had never thought he looked all that green.

Bruno was a beefy kid with a buzz cut and the same olive complexion as Luigi's. But that was where the similarities ended. Luigi felt everything with his heart first. Bruno went with his gut—or sometimes his fists.

Chester was the brains of the group. He had brown hair and perpetually puckered lips, as if he were waiting for a fish to kiss him. Chester loved tearing apart gadgets and gizmos so he could dream up his own. In that way, he was a lot like Luigi's dad.

Up on the fourth floor, piano music wafted out an open window. Luigi's little sister Arianna was practicing again.

"Is that Beethoven's 'Für Elise'?" asked Chester.

"Yeah," said Luigi. "Arianna's very talented. Her piano teacher says everyone has a gift, and Arianna's is music."

"I could never play the piano," said Bruno. "On account of my hands. They're the size of canned hams."

"Hey," said Luigi, "either of you guys ever heard of Chad Chiltington?"

"Uh, yeah," said Bruno. "His old man runs the bank. Wouldn't give my pops a loan when he wanted to open up a second butcher shop. The rich are the only ones who ever get richer. The rest of us? Forget about it."

"Actually," said Chester, "I think, if we use our heads and work hard, we can all become millionaires."

"Yeah, right," said Bruno. "Like that's ever going to happen."

"Hey," said Luigi, "we might even become bajillionaires!"

Another window creaked open on the fourth floor. The boys looked up to see Luigi's father. He jabbed two fingers into the corners of his mouth and shrieked out an ear-piercing whistle.

"Dinnertime! Tomasso, Mary, Fabio, Francesca . . . all of you. Come home! Dinnertime."

Bruno chuckled and shook his head. "Does your father even know all your names?"

"Someday, I guarantee he's going to know mine," Luigi comically proclaimed before heading inside for the family's Sunday midday meal. "I am going to be the most famous Lemoncello of them all. Who knows? I might even be the world's first bajillionaire!"

WHAT IF YOU COULD LEARN *EVERYTHING* JUST BY EATING JELLY BEANS?

MEET THE SMARTEST KID IN THE UNIVERSE AND FIND OUT IN THIS FUN-PACKED NEW SERIES BY CHRIS GRABENSTEIN!

"Clever, fast-paced and incredibly funny — Chris Grabenstein has done it again."—**STUART GIBBS**, *NEW YORK TIMES* **BESTSELLING AUTHOR OF *SPY SCHOOL***

"It's pure jelly-bean-enhanced entertainment and a perfect escape. . . . A rollicking good time."—***THE NEW YORK TIMES***

★ "Packed with wacky hijinks." — ***BOOKLIST*, STARRED REVIEW**

★ "Grabenstein delivers once again." — ***SCHOOL LIBRARY JOURNAL*, STARRED REVIEW**

CHRIS GRABENSTEIN

is the *New York Times* bestselling author of the hilarious and award-winning Mr. Lemoncello's Library, Dog Squad, Smartest Kid in the Universe, and Welcome to Wonderland series, *The Island of Dr. Libris, Shine!* (coauthored with J.J. Grabenstein), and many other books, as well as the coauthor of numerous page-turners with James Patterson, including *Katt vs. Dogg* and the Jackie Ha-Ha, Treasure Hunters, and Max Einstein series. Chris lives in New York City with his wife, J.J., and their cats, Luigi and Phoebe Squeak. The Dog Squad series was inspired by the life of Chris's late dog and best four-legged writing partner, Fred. Visit Chris's website for trailers, photos of Fred and the cats, and more!

ChrisGrabenstein.com